THE RUGGED RED JOURNEY

JOURNEY

of a prosperous and successful orphan

Chars Brown

iUniverse, Inc.
Bloomington

THE RUGGED RED JOURNEY of a prosperous and successful orphan

iUniverse books may be ordered through booksellers or by contacting:

iUniverse
1663 Liberty Drive
Bloomington, IN 47403
www.iuniverse.com
1-800-Authors (1-800-288-4677)

ISBN: 978-1-4759-1165-7 (sc)
ISBN: 978-1-4759-1166-4 (e)

Library of Congress Control Number: 2012909437

Printed in the United States of America

iUniverse rev. date: 5/24/2012

Chapter 1

It was a gloomy and cloudy day, but not cold at all, Pak Moi woke up and was about to take a shower, when suddenly there was a knock on the door, who the hell could it be this early he wondered, with no clue on what time of the day it was since he had not looked at his watch. Considering the night before he and his friends had had a blast and as far as he was concern he didn't expect to see anyone who could just come up to his place and knock on his door to be up that early, since in fact any one that was that close to him would still be in bed recovering from the blast of the night. Pak for his part thought of himself as the energy man since he was always on the go, referring to himself most time as the running man, informing his colleagues that he only slept ninety minutes out of a given twenty four hours day, he was up this early because he had acknowledgements and thank you messages to send out for the huge success from the festivities of the previous night.

As he drag himself to the door struggling to contain his fatigue and frustration for this early unwanted guest. "Who is it?" He inquired, from the other side of the door came an unrecognizable voice yet so familiar.

"You'll find out if you could just open the door."

The voice kept hitting him so strong and to his surprise he could not bring himself to put a face to the voice, finally with just three feet from the door, he was able to say "just a minute" as he regain composure and fumble with the door knob he still could not connect this voice to a face, finally as he opened the door he realize that this was the last face in the world he had expected to see, considering their last encounter. Not in a million years did he think she would ever surface in his life. Her lips parted in that familiar broad smile. "Surprised?" Before he could answer her,

"Would you invite me in?" again just as he was about to say another word, she advanced and like an unspoken command, he stepped aside open up the door and she walked pass him making her way to the center of the room saying; "I did not want to be a part of the never ending entourage you were entertaining last night, that's why I decided to stay away and have a one on one time with you when you are a little bit free and can devote some time to me too." She walked as if she was headed for the John, and knew where she was going, when suddenly she turned around and faced him, "Congratulations!!! on a job well done you've always had it in you, since the very first time

I saw you, and now you've got almost everyone else eating out of the palm of your hands, you will forever remain the most admired man in my life I really want you to know that." Just as she was ending her sentence, he found his voice, and even she was surprised at the tone, not because it was offensive rather it was more direct and mature unlike in the past.

"How did you find me; and where have you been for the last eight years?" disregarding his question she said, "I know you're not still mad at me, just like you said it has been eight years and I seriously apologize."

Amm is her name, they had a brief affair a while back, and she was one of the very few that he remembers, from a barrage of females that he had had, which means, she also has a special place in his heart, because for those who knew Pee Em also knew that he never dated any one female at a time, most knew him to be the man of no commitment where romance was involved. Every day brings a new adventure, but when it came to Amm, things were a bit different, there were some degree of emotion and deep seated passion, to him she was special, not even he could explain why, he just knew it was that way and he did not have control over that.

Pak Moi had his way with people, and he could steal his way into your world before you know it, ladies admired him highly and guys wanted to be in his position, a situation that he was well aware of and did not take lightly nor did it give him a big head, he was rather cautious about it. Since his graduation from college he put himself in the habit of not writing two letters for his initials he usually spelled out his initials as a result, for those who were not close to him or hardly knew him thought that was his full name considering it was only one alphabet short of his full name.

The first time he saw Amm he walked up to her; captivated by her beauty, he introduced himself thinking she would be moved by his charm and pretty boy appearance, she responded in a cold and not too inviting voice not even giving him her name. It turned out as popular as he was, she had never heard of him, at least not that she could remember. When he requested her name, she just said in a cold voice Amm as she walked away not being rude or anything but because she was already on her way to undertake an important venture, so she respectfully excused herself as she walked away.

Two days after, on a warm sunny afternoon they ran into one another at the supermarket, he immediately sparking a conversation, after greeting her.

"What are you looking to buy?" he asked

"A present for my boyfriend's birthday" she replied.

With a little jealousy, he said "lucky guy" not really wanting to hear another word about the boyfriend, but it kept the conversation going and it was a sense of relief to know that she had a boyfriend, where should there be a chance of any relationship between them there won't be any room for commitment on his part he could always refer to the boyfriend.

"Forgive me he heard her say, I can't remember you name"

"P.M." he called out before she could end the sentence.

"My boyfriend's sister is coming in and I think she is looking for me, I had asked for her assistance earlier in picking out a birthday present for him." As she broke into a broad smile looking pass him, he turned around to observe the excitement that befell her, his eyes fell on another remarkable beauty, with an oval face and light brown eyes, jet black hair trimmed and groomed real short, she weighed about a hundred and ten pounds, five feet five inches tall. Her steps made her appeared like she was an inch elevated from the ground that she walked on, as beautiful as she appeared he was not lusting after her as he did with Amm.

They both followed her with their eyes until she reached where they were, Amm voice at that moment brought Pak to turn and face her once more, and that was when he noticed her hand stretched out.

"This is Meik, my boyfriend's sister." Pak reached out and acknowledge the hand shake that was awaiting him.

"I did not get your name," she said with her hand still in his.

"P. M and the pleasure is all mine to be in your company and presence." With her eyebrows raised as she absorb the name, she suddenly heard herself say in a question,

"Do you mean P.M. from the P&D Arts and Publications Inc?

"Yes" he replied.

"I've heard a lot about you and never in my life had I thought I would ever run into you in this location and manner, the supermarket of all places"

"What is wrong with the supermarket and also just as a means of information don't believe whatever it was that you heard, I say this because, there is a lot of fabrication going on around town, and most people don't even know what they are talking about."

"Don't get me wrong it was all good, you are considered a legend of what you do best, Your Firm I heard has risen to the peak of the most pronounced pr firm in this city and everybody is soliciting your collaboration when it comes to publicity."

My point exactly, they're trying to set me up for failure, and when it all happens, in the end they will be the same ones to say where the hell is he now? I highly appreciate the complement coming from you, but there are firms out there that are more potent and highly profitable as compared to our young and struggling firm, I must admit though, we make the best out of what we have because we believe in striving for success"

When he had finish speaking, the two young ladies looked at each other as if singling to the other we need to do what the world we are here to do and get on with our mission in this location, after that brief exchange, Amm finally in a very polite and calm voice, bid Pak fare well and he in return replied likewise as he one last time turned to the two young ladies, and said "remember girls to have all the fun you can at the birthday party and don't do what I would not do."

Pee Em walked through the store to the check out with the bottle of wine he had picked up for a friend who he had promised because of a favor she had done for him the morning before. It turned out to be that was his reason for going into the City Supermarket in the first place.

City Supermarket is the largest department store in Boosuk, it was even equipped with a huge grocery and fresh produce section, and because of the service it provided to the community, it was always jam packed with shoppers, but for some odd reason on this day, it was pretty less busy. As he walked approaching the checkout counter, he was doing the best he could to stall his arrival in anticipation of the two young ladies catching up with him for one quick and last chat, but to no avail. It turned out to be a good thing that his wish did not come to pass, since he already had a plate full of chores.

Going through the revolving exit he heard his name, and to his relief it was his best friend and business partner Debb Rozk

Debb is bi-racial Mother German and Father African who was born to a wealthy back ground, and highly cultured in his upbringing, and like Pak six feet tall with the physical body of a Greek god with a workout schedule of at least thirty minutes a day, while making sure he can support his weight of one hundred and ninety eight pounds

Chapter 2

As the two ladies walked away from Pak Moi they waited until he was out of earshot, it was Meik who broke the silence, when she said I had no idea you were friends with Pee Em, Amm replied "he's not my friend I recently met him, and could not even remember his name." At first Meik thought she was only joking because his was a house hold name, and when, she found out that it was not a joke ,she went on to tell her that she had had a crush on him for a while but had never been opportune to be in the same location with him at any time and that she would love to have another encounter with him that could be instrumented by her, and she said "the next time I run into him I will do everything I can to hook you both up, in the main time, could you help me pick out a nice gift for my Sweetheart?" Amm and Meik picked out a Jacque Françoise matching Shirt and Tie, as they walked to the check out Meik's best friend Jazie walked in, Jazie was one who's easily noticed whenever she's around because of her loud talk and no nonsense attitude, she was also a go getter, she always brought life to the most boring gathering, she was an articulate and very observant person, a character that earned her the nick name private eye among friends, admirers and well wishers, but on the other hand to those who did not like her, very well, Miss busy bee, not that she cared so much because like she always said "you only get to know you really are alive when you have certain people for no apparent reason constantly talking about you, and don't like you because you are living your life the way you best know how and half of the world grades you excellent, twenty five percent grade you very good, fifteen percent grades you good and ten percent grades you fair or poor that lets you know that you are an influence in many lives." Jazie who had been friends with meik for her entire life was no different from her in height size and weight except in beauty where she had a round face and a black mole the size of a pea on the left side of her nose which really made her even more beautiful.

As she approached the two ladies the first words that came out of her mouth.

"Did you Girls see who just walked out of here?" Before she could say another word, Meik replied "you mean Pee Em?" They were both surprised at her "No!" answer, and when she said "your brother just walked out he was going through the exit doors while I was coming through the entrance." They both looked at one another as if they had just seen a ghost. When finally Jazie broke the silence "are you serious, was Pee Em really in here a while ago, did any one of you talk to him?" It was Jazie's turn to be surprised when Meik told her she had been introduced by Amm as she walked in the store and found them locked in a conversation. There was surprise delight and disappointment all in one from the look on her face. "I wish I was here she said turning in the direction of Amm, is he your Friend?" "I only met him a couple of days ago and before then I hadn't heard about him, what actually does he do? Since both of you seem so much interested in him and you expressing your long time crush on him." "No I did not I only said I had heard a lot about him and he knows I'm telling the truth, because for the past eight months he has been topping the chart in the in the business community when it comes to promotions every company wants him to feature an ad for them and he does it so well they all want monopoly over him but no one wants to pay the cash to foster the monopoly so he's doing what he does best and taking small contracts here and there."

"Good for him," said Amm he might make it big one of these days as she changed the subject. "Did you really see Teizo in the store before you came in?" Teizo is the name of Meiks brother the one Amm is currently dating he's with the national news network a journalist by profession in his early thirties, five feet six inches tall chubby guy who weighs about two hundred thirty three pounds, one can see that he's not the athletic type but make no mistake he was very smart and a master at what he did, when he wasn't out collecting news materials and questioning residents and tourists for his next column or editorial he could be seen at one of the famous sports bar or restaurant, but never at a night club because as far as he is concern, the school kids had taken over the night clubs that he used to two years ago.

The eight years that he had spent with the national network the students come to these places with a lot of immature act, and that it's just not worth his time spent at these places, and there were quite a few upscale and elaborate ones which were always jam packed. Every day in Boosuk appeared like a holiday one reason why tourists are never bored with the City.

Jazie nodded in affirmation to Amm's question, alas she said "I'm glad we did not run into him that way he would have been curious about our mission in here and I didn't want him to know what he was getting before his birthday," which had been schedule to be celebrated that Saturday, and it was only Tuesday but she wanted to make sure that everything was bought and wrapped even before Thursday of that week because there will be a lot going on, Friday and Teizo was a man of many friends and no enemies. This was so hard to believe, him being a seasoned journalist and loved by any and every one that he came across, it was all because of his reporting, his interest was never objectivity, rather it was human interest, developments, gatherings that were only concern with peaceful activities and entertainment. Now, one can see why he had a green light to every entertainment location in the city, because he could have your establishment out there in no time, once he started visiting. There were some owners who even went to the extent of soliciting his advice as newcomers to the scene one that he gave free of charge and not thinking anything about it.

As they walked out of the super market, everyone in their private thoughts

Meik broke the silence, "when can we set up the rendezvous, to meet with Pee Em?" Amm replied, "I have no idea I don't even know this guy let alone know where to meet him, I've only seen him twice in my life and could not even remember his name had it not been for you two, I would have forgotten about him the moment he left our presence so I won't make any promise, but I'll try to remember the next time I run into him again by chance. By the way which one of you really has the crush on him since you're both so eager to meet him?" Like a rehearsed choral group they both went " it doesn't matter" just make the contact" As the trio burst out laughing after what had just happen, Amm said "well excuse me I did not mean to offend you ladies just wanted to know before I open my big mouth to your knight in shining armor."

Meik then said "I've got an idea he could be at my Brother's Birthday Party this week end, and if he is, that could be a good time because one thing I know everybody who is somebody will be at this party so let's make it a plan to do it when we all get there." Amm cut in right away, "I just want you ladies to know that that's my Baby's Birthday, and I won't be there looking for your Pee Em, should we all be in the same location at the same time I will let him know that someone has a serious crush on him and would like to have an audience with him, and the first one that is closer will be the one to be led to him, I think that's fair enough since you both are competing for his attention we'll do it on a first come first serve basis" she said jokingly, as the three young ladies parted on their separate ways Amm took off by herself in a cab headed toward home while the other two drove in the opposite direction in Jazie's Car with Meik behind the wheel.

Almost three and a half miles to her final destination, the Taxi Amm was in blew a tire and the driver had to get out and change the tire or get another cab driver to take her the rest of the way, and she decided she was in no hurry and that he could take his time and change the tire and she would wait for him. She got out to allow him less weight in order to perform what he needed to accomplish his task since she was sitting in the back seat on the passenger side of the taxicab, that's when she noticed a photograph that she thought look familiar but on the dash board of the Cab, she did not say a word until the driver got through with changing the tire and told her to get in and that all was set and ready, as she closed the door before he turn the key in the ignition, she asked, "Who's photograph is that?" The driver immediately replied that's "My Buddy Pee Em, a very friendly and nice individual, he also runs a very organized public relations firm down town.

"How well do you know him?" She asked.

"He's a very good friend," he replied.

"A lot of people must know this guy," she said.

"That's because he knows how to treat people, and when you treat people with respect, everyone tend to treat you with respect."

"You are right," as they approached her destination.

She disembarking the taxi, and told him "keep the change" as she paid him.

"Thank you," he said.

"Will you call me a nice person too?" She joked, he just smile and said "for the few munities that I've spent with you and the manner in which you treated me I can definitely call you a nice person." She waved at him as he honked his horn.

Meik and Jazie pulled up to a red light in the heart of town, when suddenly Meik said, "speak of the devil" looking across the street in the direction of a local restaurant, before Jazie could say.

"What?" Her eyes fell on the two men making their way to the entrance of the restaurant. As they both resisted the temptation to follow them in, Meik said

"We already have it set for this weekend no need to rush; besides the guys could be going in there to conduct business and that won't be a pleasant time for any kind of social call."

The two ladies drove off to continue what the next item on their agenda for the day was, which off course included making sure that everything for the Brother's Party over the week end was on point.

Jazie was the one who finally spoke as they approached the hall where the event was to be held.

"Are they going to be the ones catering for the event, or do we have to have someone else to do that?"

"As a matter of fact I think they gave us a great deal on the rental considering that we did not have to pay a security deposit, and they've also volunteered to clean up after we leave as long as we are out of there no later than three thirty." Meik answered

Good deal Jazie said who is this guy again? Referring to the owner of the establishment.

His name is e----r, I can't remember but it's such a common name just give me a minute and I'll tell you, but I think we got a good deal because he and my Brother go way back, and according to him it will be his contribution to the Birthday Boy Meik said

What's the capacity of the hall? Asked Jazie

Six hundred and seventy five I was told.

That's not bad as they pulled to a halt and exited the car.

The name is Nige, she lamented as they walked toward the entrance of the building, I

Don't know why it just slipped my mind and I have been talking to this guy everyday for the past four days Meik said

Well it's a good thing that you remembered it before we got inside the building, can you imagine going in there and not knowing who to ask for or better yet just say I'm looking for the owner and then someone says which one?

Jazie teased.

"Wait a minute are there more than on owner?" Meik asked

"I don't know I'm just speaking hypothetically," replied Jazie as they walk up to the information section of the hall.

They went in and told the lady behind the counter why they were there and the lady pulled out a brown manila envelope handed it to meik and told her all she had to do was bring it back the next day with the signature of who will be responsible for the party should they need any information on how they will be running the event that weekend and should there be any special request for the seating of guests by the host.

After receiving the envelop the two went through the lobby to where they had parked before going into the building when suddenly as they were about to open their respective doors and be seated Jazie remembered that she had to pick up some clothes that she had dropped off at the five hour laundry a block down the street and it had been there for at least two days and since she was right down the street, it would be best for her to just pick them up since she wasn't really sure whether they would be around that side of town again before the end of the business day, I think I'd better go get my clothes from the dry cleaning while we are here, because there is no telling whether we'll be back on this side of the Globe again before the day is over, considering all we have to do with the little time the day has to offer." Jazie said

"Thanks a million for reminding me Jazie, I almost forget I do have to drop an invitation off at the cleaners, I told the lady about three weeks ago that I'd be there personally to drop it off, I guess this is a good opportunity for that"

The Duo drove to the Peninsular Dry Cleaners a block away where they performed the duties for which they had gone there and were also informed that Amm had passed by the day before to drop off an invitation to the same event, that's when Meik realize that she and Amm had discussed it the day before and that Amm did tell her that she was on her way there at that very moment because they were the two main players in the planning of this whole surprise Party in honor of Teizo.

The following day just around noon Meik and Amm were at the hall to deliver the Package obtained the following day from the facility after being singed and necessary requirements performed to enhance the conclusion of the deal for the usage of the hall.

After that the two ladies spent the rest of the week putting finish touches on every detail for the Event of the week end ahead, including the platform to get the birthday Boy to the location without giving away the surprise they had in store for him. It turned out that was the hardest thing they had to come up with, without him knowing, because he was well known and they didn't want him to have any hint before the time arrived which off course was the reason why they all decided not to send out RSVPs, because that was one way a whole lot of people would be talking directly to Teizo and telling him how they'll be at his Party, and to this point they had done very well keeping it a secret from him since everyone they mentioned it to they made sure to tress how it was very important for the birthday Boy to be kept in the dark until the moment arrived. It seemed as though everyone that was let in on it really wanted to see what his reaction would be, because remember this guy is everybody's friend ninety nine percent if not one hundred percent all the time and for some reason everyone wanted to make him happy not by trying to ruining the surprise that laid ahead for the honorable son of the Land.

Finally the decision was for Nage to make an arrangement for Teizo to meet him at the hall around eleven fifteen that Saturday for a huge fund raiser that was to be held in his honor for less fortunate kids in the community, since in fact that was his passion. Teizo was doing everything he possibly could in his writings to give voice to the voiceless which as a matter of fact he actually always said it was no fault of their own instead he blamed it on Society and the evil hand that it dealt these "Pearls of Tomorrow" as he so often referred to them. And just as they had planned it when Teizo got the message from Nage, even though he had wanted to spend a quiet and relaxing time at home on that particular evening of the week, he jumped to the invitation, for what could be so rewarding for him to be a part of a cause so dear to his heart, he accepted with no reservation.

By nine thirty Saturday Morning, a reminder was sent to Teizo for the meeting of eleven fifteen that evening, to which he confirmed his willingness to attend and expressed his excitement for a cause so worthy even the Lord God of host would be honored to be a part of, making sure that all Ts are crossed and all Is are dotted by three o'clock that afternoon Amm was with Teizo spending quality time with her sweetheart boosting his confidence and lifting his spirit for what was ahead of him the evening to come which as far as he was concern, had to do with his meeting with Nage, because he had never really stopped talking about it since the day he was approached by Nage about the meeting. We all now know her intentions were not the same as Teizo's, she was there to make sure of his attendance that evening and that the cat is not let out off the bag before the surprise of the night. Where he Teizo would be the most honored and surprised guest of the evening.

As the two Love Birds were wrapped into one another's company for the day, Meik and her Best Friend Jazie occupied themselves with the final preparation for the festivity and excitement of the evening ahead.

At six o'clock that evening Teizo and Amm went for a walk to get some fresh air, before the events of the night start to unfold, while out walking, it was Teizo who initiated the conversation. He said " you know Amm, you have been a great part of most things that I do in recent times, you never seize to amaze me the way you support the things that I believe in and for that I really want to thank you from the bottom of my heart I really mean it, because I know that I get impossible to put up with sometimes, but you have always been very much in my corner when it comes to the things that I care about, you are such a beauty and you're very smart and intelligent, I know all the men in this town and beyond will be lining up if an ad was to be put up letting people know that you were looking for a partner, I just want you to know that you will always remain in the part of my heart that no other person has and will ever see, and to let you know how much that means to me," he abruptly went down on his right knee bringing her to an instant halt as he spoke the words "Please marry me" as he reached in his pocket and presented her with a three carat diamond ring.

As the tears fell down her checks, to him it seemed like eternity, and for her one doesn't know whether she was choked on words or she was giving herself chance for the tears to fall before she could answer when finally he spoke "just don't say no anything else would be better as long as you don't say no, even if you have to defer you answer let it not just be in the negative, because if it is," as he was about to utter the next word he heard her say "yes" between the tears as he slipped the ring on her finger when two more "yes yes" rang in his ears as she helped him to his feet and gave him a big hug first then a huge and long kiss in the mouth followed by another "yes" and one final hug, as she concluded "how long have you been planning this? Because I would not have thought of this even if I was told by someone else in advance at least not today of all days" she finally said as she wiped away the tears from her eyes. In response he said I just wanted you to know that I have thought of this since the first time I laid eyes on you but I wanted to make sure the time was right before I made my move, and since today happens to be one of the best days of my life I wanted it to be yours too at least if you really see me as I see you, so we can both put what we have into the next gear until we're satisfy with what is desirable of this relationship from both of us."

After that ordeal they both went back to Teizo's apartment to start preparing for what was ahead of them, with regards to the events of their lives together and the events of the evening, which of course bear two different platforms for both of them as well, for him it was a meeting with Nage and for her it was the surprised birthday party which unlike his surprise for her that only he knew about, everybody else except him knew, and now more than ever before she really wanted it to be a true and real big surprise, since again they expected a record crowd to be at the gathering that evening.

Amm left Teizo's around eight forty five despite repeated pleas for her to stay until it was almost time for him to go to his meeting with Nage, she fabricated things that had to be done for her Grandparents before the next morning, promising that she would meet with him after his meeting with Nage and they could spend the night together which he finally gave in to. Off course she had to go home and get dressed for the event of the night. She hurried home got dressed and went to the hall around ten forty five to join everyone else as they waited for Teizo, who was to be picked up and escorted to the rendezvous location by Nage's chauffeur, who had already left to go and pick him up for the meeting/surprised birthday party depending on which party one was talking to. At Eleven ten the lights in the hall went out while Nage was seated in the front office of the building to wait for his Guest to join him as they plan and put ideas together for the big honoring bash that was to be held in his honor, it was eleven thirteen when the car pulled up and it's occupants disembarked headed straight to the front office where Nage was seated awaiting his Friend and Guest.

"Glad you could make it Teizo" as he got out of his seat to greet his guest.

"I'm highly gratified that you could even invite me for such honor, Lord knows words alone are inadequate to express my appreciation to you for such generous venture and I will always cherish just the thought of gesture," Teizo replied as he was motioned to the seat across from Nage. "Would you like something to drink?" He asked his guest.

"Some water for now thanks a lot"

He got him a bottle of processed water and said to him "Let's walk to the Ballroom where we can sit and continue our discussion."

Upon entering the ballroom, Nage reached for the light switch to turn on the lights, just as the lights flipped on with the cheers of loud noise shouting out "surprise" and party balloons going all over the place, Teizo was holding tight onto the left side of his chest as he collapsed and fell in front of the entire town, into a coma that he never recovered from. He was pronounced dead on arrival at the hospital.

It was at the funeral that Amm really came to realize that with all the grief and anger that she was going through she could not help but notice Pak's focus had never left her, in a way she herself could hardly imagine while all the other girls were craving his attention, a feeling that made her very uneasy and frustrated because not only was this guy Teizo's friend he was also Meik's greatest crush in the world as the thought crossed her mind she also factored in the part where it would be good for her to now hook him up with Meik, but then again she also noticed how he had paid her less and less attention at the entire event, with every effort she had made to try and get his attention, he totally ignored her she still could not control it and worst of all this guy was her ex fiancé's sister's dream man even though she too found him very handsome and attractive like all the other ladies. A week after Teizo's funeral Amm ran into Pak down town at one of the local restaurant, he offered to treat her that day and she accepted with the intentions of talking to him about Meik, when some way somehow he stole his way into heart and the rest is history, all Amm could think of as she walked away from her initial session with Pak, was she would one day do her best to explain to her deceased Boyfriend's Sister that she did not mean to betray her, because when she first met Pee Em, she really had no feelings for him but somehow when she sat face to face with him she was taken over with Lord knows what and just could not help but see him in a whole different respect, never in her wildest dream had she ever imagined that the man her deceased Boyfriend's Sister was so head over heels in love with was going to be the one on her top priority list of romance, and as uncomfortable as it made her feel she still didn't feel she was ready to turn him loose to her either, because when it all comes down to it he was not seeing her neither had ever express any desire for her even to the point where during their conversation every time she try to mention Meik, Pak would down play it like he was not interested in hearing about her. Especially when she specifically revealed her crush on him he directly said "I'm not at all fond of her, yes she's very beautiful and attractive, I am just not in to her like that I hope you don't think of me as a mean individual. But what good is it to lead someone on when you know you really don't care for them? In my mind I think that is the most injustice one human being can render to another especially so when it comes to romance, you want to have a romantic session with someone that you really care about, not somebody that you sympathize with, because romance is not to reciprocate sympathy rather it is to pleasure the parties involved and allow them to yarn one another's company. It seems as though as soon as those words were uttered, the sense of guilt that had crossed her mind earlier just flew out of the window, and that was when she decided that if she ever met her ex-Sister-in law she would do the best she could to make her understand and make it plain to her that it was not a betrayal, rather it was a hidden desire that she herself didn't even realize she had not that she would understand but she would have clarified the air by justifying her actions about taking Pak away from her, and that it was not done on purpose.

Chapter 3

Pak Moi, grew up never knowing his biological Mother, since she died when he was only seven months old, and above all there was not a single photography of her anywhere around he only came to know her as Pehdus, and worst of all, the Woman he came to know as his mother was not even a blood relative she had only taken over his well being because of a brief friendship that existed between the two women who came to cherish a relationship so brief yet very intense and sincere that could not be over emphasized. Unfortunately for the young Pak, all of this was made known to him at an early age, simply because the man of the house saw this little child as a treat to himself or his biological children that he had had with some other woman who no longer shared his life with him, a set of twin that were almost in their teenage years but were still behaving like infants and this little child who was only about six years old with no known background so full of life humble, kind and gentle exhibited a great deal of maturity and a high degree of responsibility, due to these attributes, almost everybody that had an encounter with this little child saw a real promising future in him, an anticipation that was very disturbing to the head of the household, because his children were nowhere near the expectations that little Pak was known to have demonstrated as a child.

Engulfed by jealousy and overwhelmed with hate for the little boy, Mr. Sojy who was known to be "head of the household and husband of the anticipated Mother" named Ninuh, would constantly remind the child when he was only five years old that his wife was not the child's mother, and that the two women met when his mother was pregnant and the two had become friends briefly before his birth never mentioning the degree of friendship, but always making show to add that they had no idea of who her relatives were or where exactly she came from before the biological Mother was killed in a hit and run accident who passed away two days after.

He was so Connie and petty about the whole thing he would wait when there was no one else around and then say to the young child "I hope you know that the woman you call Ma, is not your Mother, and I'm definitely not your Father; my wife and I are only taking care of you because your Mother did not tell her or anyone else where she came from and who her relatives were for this reason we are stuck with you and don't know who to turn to when it comes to where to take you" but with all these evil things he was saying to the little child when people are a round he would be a completely different person he would act like this little child meant the world to him and that his life had a whole new purpose because this sweet and charming little one had become a part of his. His wife Ninuh on the other hand never said anything to the young Pak and had no idea he was being told these horrible things with regards to his Mother, for as far as she was concern the child was and will always be hers, for this and other unexplained reasons thus far, she treated him like her own since in fact she had never had a child of her own and her friend before her death had told her that she regarded her as the sister she never had.

Pehdus and Ninuh first met at the Annual National Festival, a celebration which stems from a tradition of farmers, politicians and village elders in commemoration of the fore fathers who then gathered to give thanks and praises to the Almighty and award those farmers who had contributed immensely to the provision and development of the Agricultural Industry of the Land with a hefty reward going to the most productive or the highest producer. A program that was climax with lots of free food music from various bands, dance troops and several other activities. On the last day of this week long Annual Festival, just before the announcement of the Grand Winner, Officials of the Land and the top three Contestants will ascend the podium and encourage young and upcoming contestants in their various capacities as farmers and politicians followed by a Grand Ball at the City Hall with a fanfare of music from orchestras and marching bands from all walks of life. It was at the encouragement speech that the two young and single women met, and from a random conversation and a brief introduction.

The two went to the ball; though they were both young and very attractive yet single who lived approximately a whole day's drive or a minimum of thirteen hours from one another, their intensions and goals like other young ladies their age were quite different a very rear occurrence. Whilst others were there in quest of partners, these two were actually there to absorb the messages and be participants in future festivities, an interest which galvanized their relationship on a professional level and led them to be one another's escort to the Grand Ball the night of the grand finale.

With every degree of personal detail out of their conversation the two Ladies became every man present at the ball fantasy, with either going home all alone despite all advances from their male counterparts. It was another eighteen months before the two will reunite again, and this time it was on Ninuh's side of town that the two ran into one another.

Ninuh thought she recognize this person walking towards her but couldn't tell for sure until they were in arms length before she called out her name.

"Pehdus, is that you? What are you doing on my side of town and didn't even care to look for me?" She inquired "I got in last evening at about ten o' clock and checked in at the Saladeen, I'm looking for the nearest variety store to buy me some basic needs" she replied, "I think I left my belongings at the Booscum Bus Terminal".

"When did you last see your luggage?" said Ninuh.

"When we changed buses in Booscum, I was told that they wouldn't know until this evening in the main time I need some things".

"We are less than five minutes walk from the nearest store, and I'm so sorry to hear that, let me escort you to the store."

Thank you that's very nice of you.

"You're welcome, but you still haven't told me what brings you to my side of town" Ninuh continued.

"I would have tried locating you after I settled down but I wanted to take care of first things first" Pehdus said. "To answer your question directly, a friend who is advocating my partnership asked me to join him and others in a business discussion on this side of town he said it will be good to start extending out of my Comfort Zone, and I thought it was a good idea, the rest is history, by the way, do you stay far from where I'm checked in?"

"About Forty Five minutes drive away" answered Ninuh as they approached the store. "This Friend of yours, are you two involved? Not that it's any of my business" she added before her friend could reply.

"No!" she said calmly, "our relationship is strictly professional, and I harbor nothing romantic for him inside either since I do not find him attractive." They went into the store, and Pehdus picked out a few things in the toiletries department paid for them at checkout counter and they left the store headed back for the Motel at which she was staying, which also turned out to be in walking distance. For a while they walked in silence until Ninuh said.

'How would you like to get together after your session with the guys?"

"I thought you'd never ask" Pehdus replied I'm positive we'd be done no later than four thirty this afternoon come by and we'll set up something."

"I should definitely be done with my errands at that time and I don't have to go all the way home before coming back, should I run into any eventuality, I ask that you give me until five o'clock," replied Ninuh.

"That's fine with me, my room number is 135."

The two friends embraced and exchanged their see you later as each went about their business for the rest of the day or at least until their next encounter, anticipated to be around the close of the day.

At four forty seven on the clock, Ninuh was in the lobby of the Saladeen Motel, just as she was about to advance to the information desk Pehdus had her hand on her left shoulder beckoning her, "Follow me this way," Pehdus said leading the way to her room.

"How was your meeting with the guys?" as Ninuh followed her newly met friend.

"It was good, and thanks for asking."

Pehdus turn the key in the door lock as she said "men will always be men, the difference between them and us really depicts Mars and Venus we are so different, sometimes it all seems like night and day. I guess that's why God is so great and mysterious creating two sexes of like image yet so diverse."

Ninuh immediately cut in saying, "why you think he made us that way, he anticipated that if he had made us exactly the same, the world would be so one sided, everyone would end up dying of boredom." As she ended her sentence, the both burst out laughing at the same time.

"Everything about men must be logical, they project so much logic until sometimes I think the forget to incorporate common sense or reasoning, they do have some really good ideas, it's just that they procrastinate a whole lot on the little things and leave out some important details. I do think that every man should spend two hours every day getting in touch with their feminine side" said Pehdus.

"Did you know all this before or is this coming about now as a result of the meeting you had earlier with the guys"? Inquired Ninuh.

"Oh! Ninuh, I'm sorry where are my manners, would you like something to drink? Not that I have a variety, but I can at least offer something. Pehdus said "No, maybe later I'm good for now, thanks anyway. This is a real nice Motel, I've never been before today, and the beds are big and real wide."

"I love it a lot" replied Pehdus "and it is not even expensive I could stay here for a month if I had to."

"Talking about staying for a month, how long are you here for?" asked Ninuh.

"A week max, but from the manner in which things are moving it might be three days, The Guys are very knowledgeable and their line of business is Cocoa and Coffee, which I think is a very lucrative venture in this day and time, we should have another meeting by nine o'clock this evening with one of the main participant who wasn't at the early meeting due to some unforeseen circumstances, but will definitely be present at tonight's, and after that we should be nearing conclusion of the entire deal." Said Pehdus.

"I hope it all goes well for you" uttered Ninuh "as a matter of fact, since we already have plans on collaboration depending on how your session with the boys ends up, I think we should meet before your departure." She concluded. Pehdus turned sharply to look at Ninuh as if to say you read my mind, but when she finally open her mouth to respond to her friend, she heard herself saying.

"You know what? "That's a brilliant idea so let's just wait and see what the final verdict would be this evening, and you need to sleep on it too and see what and how we could go about it." "Deal?'

"Deal." Replied Ninuh.

With that the two observed a brief moment of silence and this time it was a knock on the door that alerted them, who is it? Asked Pehdus Housekeeping, came the answer from the other end we were told that you need extra linens the voice continued.

"Thanks, but I'm okay" she replied without opening the door.

It was Ninuh who spoke after that. So, what have you been up to in the social circle since we were last together?" Ironically, they were both still single, yes a fling here or there but nothing serious, it actually it's been almost two months, I'm talking about my last fling, he was nice, but made it quite clear that he didn't want anything serious, because according to him he moves about too much and he doesn't want to have to worry about anyone just as he doesn't want anyone worrying about him he was so much fun and yet very direct we spent an entire weekend together and I truly respect him for his honesty" said Pehdus in response to her friend's question.

"What about you?" she asked in return.

"There is this guy Sojy, fresh out of a relationship, been chasing me for about a month wanting to meet, he seems nice but I have not given him the requested audience, I might give him a try" said Ninuh.

Finally we are adding some spice to our meaningful lives instead of just trying to antagonize our male counterparts in a world where they seem to be so dominant.

The two ladies met around eleven o'clock the following morning, Ninuh could sense the displeasure on Pehdus face which, she did not hesitate to translate in to her voice as soon as they sat and started to talk.

"Pehdus, men are just hard to grow up, even when there is something very serious to undertake they will always try to deviate and make room for the satisfaction of the craving of the flesh, and seriously because of that I don't really think I want to partner with them." Said Ninuh, "What Happen, were they trying to make a pass at you Pehdus?" Her friend asked.

"At least two out of the group, I tell you what I will do, I'll continue with everything as planned and when the time comes for us to deposit our respective resources, that's when I'll tell them that I think I need to hold off for now and might try to join them in the future if they still think of me as a potential partner. In the main time we need to start planning what exactly we will venture into, because like I told you, they are going into cocoa and coffee, and for the brief moment I shared with these folks they really know what they are talking about when it comes to that. So since we are also trying to rival the guys, we need to know what the hell we are doing, or else the guys will bury us before we even start our journey."

"What then are you suggesting that we do?" Ninuh asked.

"What are you really comfortable with us doing,? Like I said I think I have a good knowledge from the Guys based on the meetings I've had with them but that was more of a theory, and if we have to do this we will be on our own which means we will have to do it real good or hire help that we will have to pay for, either in kind or goods" Pehdus replied.

There was a brief silence which was broken by the words of Ninuh, "when exactly are you expected to leave town?"

"As a matter of fact I'm supposed to leave town by tomorrow because we have another meeting in Booscum the day after to finalize everything we've discussed and present whatever amount we can come up with and this contact in Booscum, will make up the rest which happens to be a huge portion of the entire deal hope all goes well. Pehdus concluded.

"Well I tell you what, by the time you come back this way I would have had something lined up and then we can get the ball rolling, I hope that will be sooner than later." said Ninuh.

"I assure you that I will be back here in less than a ten days from today because I'm very serious about this, and if we both put all we've got into it, there will be no room for failure, but first we must do everything we can to eradicate mistakes that could lead to failure that's the main reason why I want to be able to meet with every player in this game just in case I decide to deviate I would be able to reference some of the encounters I'm now privilege to be a part of." Pehdus said.

"Before you leave I want you to know that the next time you're back in town I would like for you to come and stay at my place, that way, you'll be able to illuminate some of the cost for hotel and the rest, you are free to stay as long as you wish." Ninuh offered.

Accepting, Pehdus remarked, "that's very kind of you, let me warn you I'm a very heavy sleeper and when I do I also accompany that habit of mine with a huge dose of snoring, one can here me snore four miles away, are you ready to put up with a guest who won't let you sleep in peace in your own house?"

She teased.

That's very comforting to note, thanks for the warning in advance, I guess we will really get along quiet well or maybe we could form an orchestra, because as for me I know very well that I do have high and low alto I'm hoping that you can provide a nice corresponding bass to keep an audience dancing and jubilating all night long. We'll also be in the entertainment business, let's also consider that partnership as well." Ninuh commented.

The duo burst out laughing and giggling as two teenage girls sharing a good and pleasant moment of friendship. After that beautiful moment, the two young women optimistic and in very high spirit, parted with the intention of reuniting in exactly ten days, to start formulating plans for what they anticipated was a busy and prosperous endeavor ahead.

It was fourteen days before the two finally met and again it was on Ninuh's territory once again as planned. Pehdus showed up at Ninuh's address, that she had acquired during the last encounter which Ninuh insisted that Pehdus kept in her possession when ever she was headed in her direction, because as she put it "I have a place that can accommodate you me and a family of four and I live alone with no child or pet." As a result, Pehdus thought she was at the wrong address when a male figure answered the door wearing no shirt at six o'clock in the morning.

"Excuse me, I'm not sure if I'm at the right address, but I'm looking for Ninuh."

The Man at the door immediately cut in. "Are you Pehdus? Yes you're at the right address, Ninuh has been worried about you, she thought you had change you mind, come on in, let me help you with your luggage, Ninuh's in the bathroom she'll be out in a minute, I came to the door because I'm expecting someone else didn't expect that you would have been here this early," as he let her in the door. "By the way my name is Sojy, and it's a pleasure to finally meet you, Ninuh has told me a lot about you and I'm very delighted that you're here and I know how happy she would be to see you, have a seat" as he motion her to a chair and deposited her suitcase next to the chair indicated, and I will get her for you. While walking to the back of the house, as Pehdus was making herself comfortable she could hear him say at the top of his voice, "Ninuh your guest has finally arrived."

The next voice Pehdus heard was that of her friend. "Tell her I'm on my way, could you please offer her something to drink in the main time please?

Sojy came back out and offered Pehdus some coffee or tea, an offer which she said she would have later.

It was another eight minutes before Ninuh came out.

"I was so worried about you and I also thought you had changed your mind, are you alright, how was your trip back here?" Ninuh inquired.

"My trip was smooth and pleasant I've been very well, and I gave you my word a long time ago, since we first met I would have told you if I had any reservations, I said we will do this together, to me you're not just a partner you are the sister that I never had and I want you to always remember that even if things don't work out the way we anticipate, for some reason we just clicked since our first meeting and I've never had that feeling with any other Individual, I just thought I let you know that before we start this journey of ours together." Pehdus indicated.

"The mare fact that you are here means a lot, and for what you've just said, you've even elevated my spirit and if that was a pledge, I would like to take this time to redirect that same pledge back at you so to that I say sisters for life." Ninuh replied, as the two embraced and exchanged their greetings to one another. As they broke away from the embrace, Ninuh again offered her tea or coffee which this time Pehdus decided to defer, and when Ninuh spoke she said "let me take you to your room, you must be tired and ready to get some rest, we've got a lot of catching up to do I would want you to relax yourself now because we have a lot ahead of us."

"I need to, for a few hours and I should be good than we can get right to business, because I'm here for us to hit the ground running." Pehdus was saying as Ninuh directed her to the room which was supposed to be hers for as long as she was there.

Pehdus was in bed and asleep in no time at all as Ninuh went about her daily chores periodically checking in on her friend to see how she was doing or whether she was awake and needed something, it wasn't until five thirty that Pehdus finally got out of bed and walked into the kitchen where Ninuh was preparing something to eat.

"Hey sleeping beauty, you're finally up, did you get a good and enough sleep, would you like anything special to eat? Just name it and it yours for the taking."

"Thanks a lot for the hospitality Ninuh, I did have a good and enough rest, what time is it? Pehdus asked.

Looking at her watch Ninuh said "Five thirty three on the dot to be exact."

"I can't believe I slept that long, I guess I was really tired and my body did need all the rest it got, sometimes we do need to listen to our body I have not slept that long for at least three years. On the line of food I really don't feel hungry but as you already know, I haven't had any food all day so I need to eat something, and I'll eat whatever you have, smells good any way, What is it?" Pehdus said.

"Baked beans and Potatoes with Gravy made of vegetables and olive oil." Ninuh replied.

"Sounds healthy and nutritious to me, and I greatly think that's a winner so count me in." Pehdus declared.

"Be ready in a second my good friend and sister." Ninuh said, turning her attention back to what she was already doing.

"I'll go wash up and brush my teeth, and will be back before you know it."

Pehdus said. "No need to rush, your meal will be here when you get back take your time I'm going nowhere, meaning I too will be here when you're done, just take your time and be back in one piece." Said Ninuh as Pehdus walked out of the kitchen.

After Pehdus refreshed herself and came out, the two ladies sat down to dinner and had a very casual conversation about their social lives, when finally Pehdus asked about Sojy, "Isn't he the one you told me about? I'm talking about the Guy who opened the door for me this morning when I got here."

"Yes, he's the one I told you about I finally decided to take him up on his offer considering the venture we're about to undertake, we could need a male muscle or two they don't have to be directly involved in the administrative aspect of what we are doing, but make sure we have them just in case there's a need for them." Ninuh replied.

"I don't know, but I really never thought of it that way none the less, to some degree I think it sounds good as long as we agree to keep them out of the administrative region of what we're doing and they are dancing perfectly to our rhythm, I'm all in, but the moment one gets out of line I won't hesitate to descend on them with my raft." Pehdus concluded in affirmation of her newly made Best Friend and Sister's decision.

"I guess it is settled then." Ninuh said.

"It is settled." Pehdus exclaimed.

"What have you been up to since we last talked? The guy you had the week end with has he ever resurfaced?

"I have not seen him since then, I hope really not to run into him again because like he said, he's not the serious type, and I wouldn't want him to feel like he's being stalked by me or I might end up feeling that way, should he just appear out of nowhere" Pehdus said.

"Pehdus," continued Ninuh, "you might need the company and support every now and then and if you just have him around for the convenience of it I don't think that will be anything bad, besides you said you had a great time with him the last time you were together, won't you like that once in a while? Above all we are talking about muscle he could end up being your muscle in disguise, if you don't say anything, I won't either."

"How about I don't even know where to find him, like I told you, he moves around a lot according to him besides it was just a fling and the understanding was highly mutual." Pehdus went on to say.

"If that is how you feel about it I'm with you, I just want to make sure that you are satisfied with whatever decision you come up with and there be no future regrets. Concluded Ninuh.

To that not for a while the two women ate in silence, and when the y finally spoke, it was Pehdus this time, who broke the silence, and it was all business once more, "Now that I'm here and we are ready to do this, what is our plan of action, how are we going to structure this baby Project of Ours, what actually do we need for the initial start?"

"I Wanted to make sure you were well rested before we got started, but since you would like to hit the ground running, I'll just let you in on what I already have going since our last meeting. I came in two days after we met and negotiated for a parcel a land, initially I was given seventy five acres, since I'm a lady, but after I hooked up with Sojy and told him to only portray to be a part of my team I was able to acquire hundred and seventy five more acres because of that we have two hundred and fifty acres to start of with and depending on how well we do and our placement in the Annual competition for the next three years we might be asked to give up some of the land that we now have, or be given more land for subsequent competitions. What we need to do at this point in time is make sure we get and we can secure more seeds to plant than we have place for, not forgetting to mention the assembly of a good bit of muscles to cultivate the land while we supply the necessary needed support for them. That include and; and not limited to, making sure to feed them every work day, making sure they're on the job on time and are actively engaged in what they are there for, this means that we will have to take them through an evaluation process before they're even on the field and once they are there make sure they are properly divided in section to their task, as a matter of fact, to make it more exciting, group them up in teams and institute competitions where they could be awarded prices as the farming season progress." Ninuh concluded her deliberation.

"You really have been busy since we last met, I must congratulate you on all you've done and continue to do I see a whole lot of progress already. I can assure you that I have not been as busy as you have, but to my knowledge I've made some significant head ways in regards to getting crops and working tools that will also enhance the physical aspect of our project, which was all made possible from my association with the Guys the past few weeks, I'm hoping that in the next few days I can have all that delivered to the most strategic location from where you have the acres secured." Pehdus continued. "By the way, are all two hundred and fifty Acres in the same spot or do we have more than one location?" Pehdus asked.

"I'm glad you asked because it slipped my mind, there are two locations, within walking distance approximately fifteen feet apart, and it's definitely to our advantage, because the fifteen feet division has a river bed that we can use for irrigation purpose." Ninuh implied.

Sincerely I don't know to whom should I attribute thanks and praises for a vision such as yours, whether your Parents for giving birth to you or the Almighty God for creating them, I guess I'll just do both anyway, since in fact you can not divorce one from the other." Pehdus remarked jokingly.

As she emptied her plate and started to reach for the glass of water when suddenly they heard the squeaking sound of the front door, that lead Ninuh to say "oh, I didn't know it was this late, Sojy is already home, I guess it's true what they say, time flies when you're having beautiful and worthwhile discussion for wealth."

"I guess so, and don't forget to power and confidence to the phrase the next time you air it." Replied Pehdus.

The weeks following their discussion at the dinner table we the most hectic for as long as they could both remember, from the scheduling of interview with prospective workers which they referred to as "muscle" to the receiving of working tools, tree stubs and seeds the days appeared to have a maximum of six hours, because there was so much to be done and the goal they had set was that everything should ready in ten days, in order for them to start preparing the land for their project by the first day of the third week in order to achieve the intended goal which means they only had four days to put finishing touches on things that were to be completed, there were times when the two women thought about giving up, but their determination was their motivation which lead to perseverance even when others seriously doubted their ability to, come to think of it, it was those skeptics who made them even more determine to continue working hard, because the time flew so fast and the job was so tiring the two ladies did not really believe how much they had accomplished until the very last day of their preparation stage.

The two women had put their hearts minds bodies and souls into what they had believed in and God knows how satisfy they were with the result thus far, even though they still had a long way to go but so far the beginning was already telling them that there was a bright future ahead, as a result they rewarded themselves with a make shift party with no guest or invitee but just the two of them and a twenty four ounces bottle of oranges juice each, with the notion that they were giving themselves a pat on the back for a job well done.

In as much as they had work so hard, even they were not prepare for what awaited them, when things got into full swing. Mother Nature cooperated so well that year with the Farmers of the Land, every desirable weather was in a great degree of compliance, a speculation which made people to start harboring the believe that it was because of the involvement of the two women that everything was going so well, and their produce turned out to be so well maintained and rich looking that the rumor was well worth it, and because of this good news, they had more people wanting to associate with them than they could accommodate, everybody was eager to be of assistance to the ladies, an offer which was utilized in the areas that it was most needed. As a result of the above, it was no doubt on anyone's mind that these ladies will definitely be front runners for the annual farmers award, because four months before the festival, judges and spectators alike came from all over the world to see what these two had done and how much they had change the views of those who thought it was not possible to achieve such remarkable success, at least not for a first timer above all these were women and the fact that no woman had taken part in this, it was next to impossible that they will do well at a first chance given them. For the next four months preceding the award festival the women were constantly the topic of most discussions in that regard.

Barely two months before the big occasion that they had work so hard for, Pehdus started feeling sick, a disturbing feeling which led her to seek medical attention, just to be told that she was expecting a baby. A declaration which made her laugh and think that the Doctor who told her that was probably drunk or on some drug, when she told him she had never missed her period since the last time she had sex and that was almost seven months past and he told her she was right because she should be having the baby in about two to three months, she wanted to know if there was anything she could do to abort the pregnancy, when she got a negative answer her heart skipped a beat, because she knew there was no way she thought she could find the man who father her child besides there was too much at stick to go to the ceremony pregnant and not knowing whether she will ever be able to lay eyes on the father of her baby, and as she had already been told, abortion would mean suicide a program he was not willing to be apart of. His best advice was, you never know what that child will turn out to be, it's best that you keep the baby because one of these days that child might be the one to be your pride and joy he finally told her, even though those were not the words she wanted to hear, but again she had no other choice and if there was any consolation, so far it has not been noticeably, and it might definitely end up being that way until the day you give birth, a line which turned out to be very true.

When her business partner/sister/best friend got the news she made the same statement with a great deal of empathy for her friend and partner, about how good her body was at covering a pregnancy that old, and just like the Doctor told her if it had not shown all this time she didn't think it would be showing by the award ceremony, her only concern was that it happened after and not before, because she knew how hard her friend had worked to witness every aspect of the festivity which was less than eight weeks away. As it turned out, just as Mother Nature had previously cooperated with the ladies in the wake of their farming and harvest seasons, again Heavens was on Pehdus side she was at the festival feeling sick on and off nothing severer, but a little uneasy, all of which was played down when they were announced the first runner up at the annual festival, next the group that she had almost partnered with, a venture and apposition that was well worth it to the women, because, now they are not only competitors, they're also recognized as a force to reckon with. As they put it a couple of female high rollers in a male dominated world being a part of the decision making body.

Exactly fifteen weeks after their big pay off, Pehdus give birth to a bouncing baby boy, whom she named Pak, and again declared to her friend and partner that it was their son, and in extreme confidence told her that, it's all because of that fling she told her about she further went on to tell her that the boy looked just like his father not that she expected to see him any time soon but one can never tell where life's journey may take you, in that they were both guest in the land which they had now made home and have been accepted part and parcel of the territory they now occupied to the extend where they were given distinguished citizens award by the authorities. With all this declaration little did she know that she was only going to live seven months into her new born son's life leaving her friend to parent him for another nine years before her death, but not before a reunion with the father and son.

It all happened for the first time when at age eight, while Ninuh was out with little Pak an attractive athletic looking gentleman approached her and asked about Pehdus at first she thought he was one of those who had seen them together in the past, and when she gave him the sad news he could not control his hurt and disbelief, that was when he revealed to her that, he had only approached her because he had seen the little boy who looked every bit like her and revealing to Ninuh that he had spent the best weekend of his life with her and had never been able to get her off his mind, but the only reason why he had not been able to reunite with her again is because they did not exchange contacts. Based on what he had told her including the time he specified, she concluded that she was looking at this little Boy's Father and didn't know it, above all how does she reveal to him that this is a his son, that is when it down on her that over the years she thought that the boy looked very much like his father simply because his mother had said it, but when this total strange told her to her face that the boy looked like her she saw every spit of her friend in the child that had now become hers. That was when she explained to him what transpired on the weekend in question and she had never had anyone else until her death, but she always made herself to believe that the child looked like the father.

Pehdus had never mentioned this guy by name she always referred to him as the fling of her best weekend ever, and even he has just reiterated the same for himself so maybe and just maybe these two were meant for one another, unfortunately she's not around to share this moment, just the thought of that made her heart to sink, it was at that moment that she told him that the boy's name is Pak and he told her that was his last name and his first name is Sandy. So that meant that the boy is his son, a revelation that he was so delighted over and could not help to express his desire to have the boy spend some time with him at her approval, a proposal which she welcomed with open heart. They exchanged contacts when he told her he was in town for a few more hours and as soon as he was back in the country he would let her know in order for them to plan it well a gesture that was pleasing to both parties.

Due to his busy schedule and his constant travel around the Globe, it would be another year before he could lay eyes on Ninuh and little Pak, but he was in constant contact with them following his every progress along the way sending them every pleasing gift he could possible get to them. Again when they met after a year the most he could spend with them before he was call to go on another tour was four days, in on Wednesday morning and had to pull out Sunday Afternoon, and this time it will be nine months again before he laid eyes on the little one at which time they spent a week together, he left with the intentions of going to secure a cabin for them to travel on a train to his home town when the sad news came back to them in less than three hours that he was instantly killed in a car crash, this time an unbelievable blow to the young Pak who was only on a journey to bond with his father and once again death has snatched it cold hands on one this major flesh and blood of his.

So now at age ten he had no biological parent alive that anyone that he was connected to knew of simply because his mother never talked about anyone on her side of the family and the father who was about to take him to meet his side of the family was gone not saying to him anything about them either. The worst scenario was yet to befall the little boy, but that would finally hit home five months before his tenth birthday when Ninuh who had been serving as his mother was diagnose with liver cancer that was in it's chronic stage, and was given three months to live but passed away five days after the diagnoses, leaving little Pak to grow up on his own.

Chapter 4

Pak, after loosing his every known and kind Parent that he had ever encountered in his young life, had become an orphan and must grow up fast, but at his age what had he accomplished to facilitate this unforeseen adventure of his?

Only God knows how he would propel himself through life's twist and turns.

Just as the thought of how the little one will deal with life's ups and downs and everyone who once knew him was trying to see what assistance he could be rendered, out came Mr. Sojy, making promises even he knew he could never keep. At first some people thought he meant well, but even little Pak knew that this man had once again surfaced in his life to create another stumbling block for the next face because he had travel this road before and had had to put up with some very unkind words from this man, now that everyone who could ever care for him is dead, what does he want? Is he coming around to make sure that nothing good comes from this Young Child, or is he trying to kill him too? Some thought, simply because all that he had caused the little Boy to endure did not stay behind close door, especially after Ninuh separated from him when she learned that he had been ill treating Little Pak, a sentiment she did not hesitate to exhibit publicly, so it was an open secret that everyone else knew about including Little Pak's deceased Father, which prompted the decision the more so to take his Little Boy Pak with him, when suddenly he met his untimely death.

Pehdus and Ninuh were business partners and based on what they had gone through, and couple together with the influence they had in the town, they had a good bit of money kept for mishaps, and for both women Little Pak was high on the list, meaning if things didn't go the way they anticipated, whatever they had set aside was definitely going to be left to Little Pak. In as much as they had all this planned, no one else had any information about what was going on, except that since Ninuh was legally married to Sojy she must have reveal their plans to him or even added him on to a legal document before things got sour between them thus prompting their separation, and since they were not divorced, things could turn out to be very crucial if the necessary provisions were not made for Pak who is still under age and will definitely need a great deal of adult supervision for at least five more years of his young life before he could start making critical decisions on his own.

As the gossip circulates around town every body has his or her own version of what has recently become the town's juicy gossip, depending on who is transmitting the gossip at the time, for some they said everything was in Sojy's name and that without him Little Pak could not get any thing, for other's he had come out of the woods to exploit the Little Child, these were the two main sayings ahead of the many other stories that were in circulation, and everyone one was eager to see what the next step would be.

Everyday brought a new version of speculation to the scene and everyday the gossip gets more traction and gain meaningless intensity, until the third month after Ninuh's death on a gloomy and cloudy morning the town woke up to the disappearance of Little Pak, an event which spark a whole new line of gossip and speculation, again with Sojy at the center of it all. This time it is so gruesome that some even thought there could be some foul play behind it all and who ever is responsible must be dealt with accordingly if and when caught.

Everybody who knew Pak and had interacted with him had some high regard for him, as he always exhibited a high degree of maturity beyond his age couple with the level of responsibility which was immediately noticed when he was locked in to a conversation with anyone, and for these characteristics love and admiration were harbored for the young child where ever he was present, but with all this high regard harbored for him no one in their right mind thought that at his age, he would be able to stir his young life into becoming a productive and conscious adult, so when news of his disappearance hit the scene, and with a speculation that there is some hidden treasure lurking some how some where with his name written all over it, some got really concerned especially so when Sojy who people once knew to have had a rocky relationship with his then separated and young Pak came out of nowhere to claim custodial duties for a child that he had once had a problem with to the extend that his marriage was placed on the rocky lane thus prompting the separation between him and his wife Ninuh, eyebrows were raised and with grave concerns too.

While the town was reeling in it's chaos and confusion and as everyone else decipher his or her encounter with Little Pak, all he wanted to do was make sure he stayed away from the town as far as he could, but being a child and with no financial potency, he did no know what he could do to achieve his wish without conveying it to someone else, above all he did not know if there was anyone so worthy of his trust that he could confide in to express what he felt, his next move surprised even himself, but as the saying goes desperation brings out the best or worst in anyone, and that's exactly what happened to little Pak when he found himself in a situation that he knew no way out of.

On the night following the morning the entire town took to the streets looking for little Pak, he knew he had to do something that no one would support him on, whether it was a good idea he really didn't know, but one thing he was sure of, was he had to get away and get away and get away fast it was that thought that led him to take the desperate measures that he'd never envisage. It was around mid night when almost everybody was in bed resting preparing themselves for the hustle, and bustle of the work day that lie ahead, when Pak stole his way from everyone and found his way to the nearest pick-up truck parked almost near the center of the town, and when he found out that he was not being watched, he hopped in the back of the pick-up truck and it turned out that luck was on his side, because as it turned out, there was a blanket exactly where he had decided to seek refuge and that blanket ended up being his shelter for two hundred and thirty miles twenty minutes after he covered his entire body with it, and since all this took place in the dark of night, not even the driver of the pick-up truck noticed anything out of the ordinary, as a result when he arrived in the City of Aberdeen, he did not border to check around, instead he headed straight for the bathroom, and that was all the time little Pak needed to break away from the location which had been his home and shelter for the last couple of hours. He jumped out of the back of the truck when he realize that the driver had disembarked and wondered of into the wee hours of the morning with no idea of where he was going and what the next item on his agenda was, but surprisingly very happy that he had left everyone and every thing that reminded him of where he came from.

Since he was already in the heart of the City of Aberdeen, where people could be easily seen sleeping around on cardboard boxes made of bed, he luckily located a spot where he fell and dosed of to sleep awaken to the sound of pedestrians and automobile, it was still early the day had not even started and it was still a little dark, but already you could see that the early birds were beginning to open their stores and while others were receiving customers. One thing stood out to young Pak, this was a much bigger and by far more populated place than where he had come from, and because of that he instantly knew his quality of life was about to take a whole new direction, just seeing how fast the pace of the environment was give him a revised energy, his young mind imagining what it would be like to grow up in this vast land of fast moving objects. Just as he was about to take a step to the closest open store with the most busy traffic he looked up a saw a Catholic priest in his red robe who nodded at him as they made eye contact an opportunity little Pak could not allow to pass him by so easily, he ran over to the priest while introducing himself, he inquired "Sir is there anyway that you can assist me in giving me a task that I could be compensated for?"

The Priest was surprised, because Father John Georges as he was known by the entire resident was so sure that he was the most popular Priest in all of Aberdeen, and he was also known by all kids that were in reach including this little boy for his generosity not just from his help for all foundation which had just a day ago extended an arm to the less fortunate but for his daily athletic programs with the little ones, so why would he come ask him for a task that he could be compensated for?

Baffled by what he had just heard, he asked, "what's your name son, and where are you parents?"

"My name is Pak Sir, and both of my Parents are deceased"

"Sorry to hear that, but where do you live?" the priest asked.

"Sir I don't know yet I might find out by tomorrow"

"With whom do you live?"

"Sir I'm here alone, everybody that I've known in my life has left me, and I have nobody in this town I'm here all by myself."

"How long have you been in this town?"

I have been hear for less than a day, and I never want to go back to where I came from, because I've had a lot of bad experience going back to where I came from will only make me to do things that I do not want to do, even though I've been here less than a day I feel very good already and I thank God that I broke away from that life."

Shocked and transfixed in the position Father Georges found himself he could not find the words he really wanted to transmit to this little Child, when finally the words came out all he said was, what can you do son that you think will help you earn your living in this big City?" He asked, and this time more amazed at the little boy's answer when it came out.

"Father, if the Lord could shelter me all the way from where I came to this point, he will definitely see me through the rest of my journey in life."

At this point, this dedicated servant of God could not help but admire this little Stranger who had exhibited such high level of maturity and confidence for his young age.

"I tell you what," said the Priest. "If you be a good boy I promise that I'll find you something that you can do that could help you, but I must at least know where exactly your relatives can be found, because you just don't know how bad it is out here."

"Sir, I don't see anything that could be worse than where I came from, I was less than a year old when my maternal Mother was killed in a hit and run accident a few days after, my Biological father whom I've seen at most three times in my life was killed in a car crash the day I was supposed to move in with him and his family that I had never seen or known, and in less than three months, the woman whom I had known as the only relative I had left on this earth died of cancer to the liver which was in it chronic stage when diagnosed."

After a brief pause he finally said, "now Sir if that's not reason enough to satisfy you, that is more than reason for me besides, I only want to get away from all the death change location and start at fresh I only hope that others will understand since they won't be able to walk directly in my shoes."

Father Georges finally had to admit this little Child, if he was revealing what had happened to him, for he had no reason to lie, he really was far beyond his age in life and it's all maybe because of the cards that life had dealt him in his young age. He thought, and his next thing he did even he did not think it was right since this little one did not have anyone around to vouch for him, but again that's why we are put on this earth to overcome adversities and this young individual has only encountered his at a much earlier stage in his young life.

"I am Father John Georges the priest for the Cathedral on Bedford Street, right now I need to pick up a few things from the Food Store across the street and if you could just walk with me there, I'll take you to the Church Compound where I could find you something to do and we see how much you might like it and that could be a start. Does that sound good to you? He asked in conclusion.

"Father I'm very pleased with your offer and I promise you will never regret for giving me this chance."

In his subconscious mind the Priest had already convinced himself that with such brilliance and maturity exhibited by this young child, he could not expect to let anything deter him from rendering him any assistance he possibly could, because for him this little one could be an inspiration for kids and adults alike, but little did he expect that there would have been a few who would think otherwise including a very close friend of his, who when told about the misfortune of little Pak, said he could be a demonic child for all you know, a statement which was disproved by little Pak as the first few days of stay with the Priest turned out to be very promising, another thing noticed by Father Georges was how much independence the Child had shown, he did not believe in hand outs, he always tried to reciprocate every courtesy that was rendered him, and if he found out that he could not do it right then and there, he would sincerely promise that one day when in a better position he would make show to do what ever he could to make you appreciate him for what you have done for him, something you did not find a lot of kids his age doing.

Pak who all he needed was fifteen seconds with anyone born of a woman to be sold on his charm and intelligence was a very modest and humble person in his adolescence never had a negative comment or a harsh word for anyone even when he was dealt the worst hostility, he was always soft spoken and he tend to choose his words carefully before directing them at who ever was on the receiving end a characteristic which made him famous and respected.

It was three weeks before school started when Father Georges first laid eyes on Pak, and the school that he was heading was neither elementary or junior high, and considering his age he knew that Pak was not yet in high school, for this reason he would have to make sure he can get him in school as soon as possible, and as he had already realize from talking to Pak and a quick test paper that he had given him he would easily pass for six or seven grade, but that he would let the school where he was accepted be the judge of It came as no surprise when Sister Gorealla who was head of the Christ the King Junior high School told Father Georges that the young Pak had passed with flying colors in every subject that he was tested, she explained to him that since there was no transcript for him from any where, she first give him a six grade test which he completed in record time thus prompting her to the next advanced class, and that he completed in a much shorter time than the previous one, and again she stepped it up one notch once again the same ability was demonstrated, and nothing changed when she tested him for the ninth grade, but in order not to waste his time and keep him far back where learning would be boring for him, she decided to place him in the eighth grade at least where he would spend two years in the Junior High School before going to High School, considering he was only eleven years old, a decision which Sister Gorealla did not even regret because by the middle of the school year Pak was once again well ahead of his classmates when he was put in the ninth grade to finish the school year when once again he came out way ahead of the class in every subject in both class work and state administered exams, even though he was not on scholarship because Father Georges made it his responsibility to personally sponsor him through this private institution, he had paved his own way to the very High School which Father Georges was heading on an full academic scholarship which included books and stipend, above all he was being housed by the generosity provided through Father Georges by the Catholic Mission stationed in Aberdeen.

With every assistance provided by Father Georges, he did not once think to pressure young Pak to adopt the Catholic Doctrine; all he told him was make sure you attend service you must help out in the usual weekly decoration of the Church Edifice for the regular Sunday Service, and break down used and unwanted decoration to be disposed of when need be. With all efforts Father Georges had made to allow Pak to make decisions on his own based on the kind of human being he had come to know Pak to be since their very first encounter Pak had chosen to follow the teachings of the Catholic Doctrine, a teaching in which he was so involved that everyone who knew him, thought he would have end up being a Catholic Priest like Father Georges. As a matter fact, some even thought he was being groomed by Father Georges to follow in his foot steps little did they know even the Priest was being constantly amused by this young one who had endured so much tragedy in his life, there had to be some very high power of Devine intervention to mould him into the extraordinary individual he had become in life. Though still young to be in the class in which he found himself at school, his comportment in life was remarkable, and Father Georges always found himself in a position where he had to defend himself against the one who's responsible for being the one driving force, little did he know that to some degree he definitely was of some influence to the boy's behavior in society.

Everything was going quite well in Pak's life until he made it to the twelfth grade then aroundthe end of the first semester on his way from school just as he was about to exit the school building he heard his name when he turned around he was starring Sojy straight in the eye, before his heart could skip a beat the thought ran through his mind, and before he could finish thinking, the words came out of his mouth and through his lips, in his usual calm and controlled voice.

"What are you doing here, and how did you find me? I thought I had turned this page in my life when I fled from you, Don't you think you have scared me enough to leave me alone and let me live my life in peace? Considering some of the awful and nasty things you told me when I was still a child and above all after the death of the only Mother that I'd ever known for you to show up out of nowhere pretending to want to be apart of my life simply because of your own personal ambition. I never did think you of all people would ever come looking for me. Again tell me, why are you here?" Pak asked.

"I truly understand your frustration Pak, and I wish one of these days you will find it in your heart to forgive me for what I put you through earlier in your very early stages in life, having said that, I 'm actually here to authenticate your existence, because after your disappearance, a whole lot of people were looking at me thinking that I had done something to you for whatever fortune that awaited you from Pehdus and Ninuh, and to tell you the truth, after Ninuh's death when I came around, I did not come because of all that, I actually came around because I wanted to make amends for all the trouble I had caused you and see how I could be of some help to you, you were so young and venerable and I thought my presence would make a difference, and I had no idea I had damaged you so badly all I can say to you now is I have no words to express my regrets for the pain that I've caused you." Sojy concluded.

Baffled by his statement Pak went on to say "since the day I left on the back of that pick-up truck, any and everything that I felt had one way or the other contributed to my short comings I ask the Lord to touch my heart and grant me a forgiving spirit, and by the time I jumped off the truck, everything was automatically lifted of my mind I have never harbored any bad notion about any individual since, so if you are only here to clear that up I gave you my word that its all been cleared off " Pak replied in his usual calm and collected tone of voice.

Sojy in turn could not help but recognize how grown and matured Pak had become over the years, and this time when he spoke it was with a lot of remorse. "I would really like to clear my name from all the gossip then and now that's the reason why when I saw the publication of your dedication to the youth community in Aberdeen I could not help but to locate you and now I've seen for myself, I must admit, I'm not at all surprise the way you turned out to be so far, you are an amazing young man and your Mother if she had lived to this day would have been a very proud Mother just as she was when she gave birth to you. You were the apple of her eyes and I think she ended up infecting Ninuh with similar love and passion. I know full well they're both in Heaven right now smiling down on you, you are God's gift to this earth, and don't you ever forget that I just wish at least one of my offspring would have turned out to be two percent of what you are, you my friend cause people to wish you were theirs, that I know you inherited from your Mother."

When Sojy ended his statement, Pak did not speak immediately, he kept starring at him until Sojy said "I will understand if you don't want to say any thing with regards to what I've just said, and again I'm grateful for your forgiveness, I just wish I could ever make things right with you as I promise you from this day forth I will do everything I can to find favor with you, even if I have to die trying I will."

For the kind of person that he was, Pak only repeated again in his usual tone I've already forgiven you and you don't have to make it up to me for any reason' I just felt that the time had come for me to move on and that's when I decided to do what I had to do, as far as I'm concerned that chapter in my life is over the memories I will forever cherish, but the agony I've already shed there is no need for bitterness because all it does, is depresses the body mind and soul, and life is too short with too many evil going on in the world today to dwell on depressing factors when life offers beautiful moments everyday to be thankful for, you can go on living you life with ease and keep thanking the good Lord just for keeping you in good health, and continue asking him to redirect the paths of your Children for only he has the power to transform the evil that we human beings effect and practice into good. Something my Father told me on the day that he died; he said we perform evil deeds because we come to know it as part of our existence and subscribe to it, which is the choice that we make but what if we all choose to go in the opposite direction things will be so much simply to handle, but that will make life very unfair because we need evil to appreciate the good so evil is part of us and we must make room for it in society, or else we would all perish from boredom, and have no concrete explanation for the causes of things around us."

In short what he was saying was, give thanks for good fortunes as well as bad situations because that's what we are made of and we will always practice the things we were made to do.

Finally, Pak said to Sojy changing the subject, "as you see I'm just leaving school I need to find something to eat, I could meet up with you later if you like."

"I've been in Aberdeen for at least six hours, and I wasn't planning on spending the night until I heard and read about you in the local papers and I wanted to make it my business to see you before I left town with that in mind I decided to see if it was the same person thus leading me to where you are, and I'm very happy that I made the attempt. I'll go check myself in the nearest hotel and we could meet before the evening is over, whatever you decide I'm willing I think we both got some catching up to do." As they were walking in the direction of the hotel, Pak said "you don't have to stay on my behalf if you've got things to do, because just as we met today by fate, we could meet again one of these days we could cross paths again in future." Without being offensive, but with a sense of relieve that he might not have to be dealing with Sojy no time soon or maybe never again. Not because he did not mean what he said about the forgiveness to Sojy instead his presence was something that perpetuated the pass and he never wanted to resurrect the demons of yesterday but he had to say it without hurting this individual's feelings, if not for anything; he has made great effort to find and pour his heart out to him for what had been done to him years back and as a practicing Christian he must exhibit what his faith depicts.

To that when Sojy finally said, "for you Pak nothing is too good, right now in this day and time if I had known what I know now, you would have been my joy and laughter just as you were for the two most remarkable women in you and I lives." At that point, they were both at the street corner, when Pak finally extended his hand for a hand shake with Sojy and said; I must be headed back to the mission where I stay, because it will soon be time for supper and I don't want to keep the others waiting, we should be done no later than seven thirty pm and I'll be in front of the school where we met earlier at eight o'clock pm and I shall see you then.

Sojy on the hand shake replied, that will be enough time for me to do what I have to do and be back here promptly, and I will definitely be here, you take care until we meet again soon.

They both went their separate ways turning and looking over their shoulders constantly as if to be sure the other is not in harms way as they waved back at one another with a sign indicating see you later.

The was something that Pak could not get of his mind, it hasn't been that long, but Sojy sure has aged a lot even though he is still recognizable, one can tell that he looks much older than his age, has he been carry all these feelings along with his deceased wife so much so that it has crept his age looking figure to where it is, or is it his kids? He thought, when suddenly his thought was interrupted with a familiar female voice, which he'd recognize to be that of Suzette, Suzette an elite of the City of Aberdeen, the City's most prestigious bakery and pastry producer is own and operated by her family, in fact it was named in her honor by her Father who happens to be a very powerful individual in the area. Suzette is a close friend of Pak, she's a tenth grader who felt head over heels since the first time she laid eyes on him, two days after he got his result from the ninth grade on his way to the tenth grade, some way some how she felt an attraction of mixed emotions, a feeling that she'd had to battle with until her first real face to face audience with Pak, which was three months after she first saw him, after that first meeting, the two instantly became friends when they realize that they had a lot of similar interest.

Chapter 5

The friendship between Pak and Suzette to everyone seemed like a match made in Heaven, since in fact it started of being mostly on the intellectual basis, but also appeared to be perceived as the odd couple with regards to their social back ground, Pak being an Orphan from nowhere and Suzette an Elite from the City of Aberdeen, who grew up in the spotlight of the City's residents and admired guests with a wealthy establishment named in her honor a very smart and beautiful young girl, in the eyes of Suzette who also was an only child and hare to the pastry empire of Aberdeen, Pak was not only a companion, he was also an idol for her pier and more; as a result her confidence in him was remarkable.

When Pak finally caught up with Suzette, like always her first question was "what's on your agenda for the day?" and as always his answer "what do you have on your mind?" Right after that usual chat of theirs, they go straight into their normal conversation. She told him how she had seen him walking with this strange individual and just wanted to know if everything was alright, he in turn who had made no secret of his past told her who the individual was and the discussion they he had had with Sojy which lead to them setting up a meeting for later on in the day, she out of concern and support for her Idol and Friend wanted to know if she could accompany him and when he declined her offer she reassured him that if he ever changed his mind she was always there for him no matter what. After which they went and join the rest of their crew to have supper a behavior which had become habitual since they decided to be a part of the progressive youth organization spear headed by Pak and Suzette as his principal deputy, for the benefit of bringing town's youth together in unity and youth development projects for the benefit of the youth growth and leadership of the City's future advancement.

Sojy on his way to book a hotel for the night kept thinking to himself how much the little boy he had known a few years back had really made a prominent and upright citizen of himself so far and looked forward to the meeting later on during the day, but first he had to find a convenient shelter for the evening because in his mind there was more to their meeting later on than they could both imagine and since he was the adult he had to prepare himself well since this was no longer the little child he once knew, for that little child had become a promising young individual and a future leader based on what he had read in the local newspapers and the brief conversation that had transpired between them earlier during the day had confirmed exactly what the print media had published about him, so on his way back to their meeting point, Sojy had to keep playing the devil's advocate in his mind anticipating what the discussion would be like. A battle that was going on in his mind which lead to his distance from reality that impaired him from knowing that he had arrived at the meeting point until he looked up and saw Pak standing approximately five yards from him with a beautiful and very attractive young lady standing next to him. Pak as usual who is known to be very time conscious, even though he was only a stone throw away from where they were expected to meet, had made it his business to arrive at least fifteen minutes before the time specified by both of them Suzette on the other had insisted that in as much as he did not want her around, he was only going to be there until his visitor arrived and she would leave to meet up with him again later on before the evening was finally over, a suggestion which Pak reluctantly give in to after her repeated insistence to at least have a real good vision in the wake of any unforeseen circumstances of this long lost friend or relative of Pak who had become and inspiration in her life.

Sojy and Pak met as planned with a more enthusiastic greeting, firmer hand shake and welcoming attitude this time around, and Pak making a formal introduction between Sojy and Suzette, a name that Sojy thought he had seen or heard many times since his arrival in the City of Aberdeen. After which Suzette excused herself and beckon Pak to make sure he got he touch with her before retiring for the evening, which he replied in the affirmative as she walked away from he and his long lost Relative and Friend.

As she walked away with her back turned, Sojy's voice ring in the air, "she's such a beautiful young lady who appears to be also very polite and respectful and her name sounds too familiar,"

"Her Parents own the most lucrative bakery and pastry business in the City which was named in her honor by her father," Pak told him. At that time it all came to Sojy why the name sounded so familiar. He went on to change the subject, "I was really amazed when I heard your name and learned of some of the positive impact you've made in this town, I could not wait to locate you, I want to reassure you again that I am very happy for you and I also want you to know that after you disappeared, a lot of people thought there was something terrible that must have happened to you, and I was looked at as the one responsible for your mysterious disappearance since it was perceived by most that there was a huge inheritance with your name all over it from both your Mother and Ninuh and I stood to gain a lot since I was still married to Ninuh before her death, there are folks back home who still think that the truth shall come out and I will end up paying the price for your disappearance. Heaven knows how happy I was when I verified that it really was you whom I have heard off, and even more delighted to learn of how much influence you have had on both the youths and adults in the community. Above all I'm so gratified that you considering what I put you through; you can still grant me an audience after accepting my apology, which I know you did not have to do in conjunction with my admiration for you I also want to register that even though I'm much older than you are, you have a far better forgiving spirit than I do and I would even say much wiser than I am at your age."

"I want to thank you for the commendation and every kind word you have uttered, but even though those were some tough times that I had to endure at your hands, I don't see them as a channel by which I should harbor negative attitudes toward people who instituted them rather I see it today as a road to solidify some or most of the good that come out of me today, in short that was a path preparing me for the adversities in my early life, as you rightly put it if that had not happened you and I wouldn't be here today, or better yet having this conversation. In as much as you thought you did me wrong, I think the good Lord made it that way for my journey through life. I don't mean to sound mean or cruel about the situation, but from the Biblical days people have been put into situation to facilitate the occurrences of events fore told, some common example include; Moses Pharaoh and the Israelites, or Jesus Judas and the thirty pieces of silver. I think Mankind should be able to commend both Judas and Pharaoh for their rolls in facilitating the inevitable. Don't get me wrong I really mean this in the most positive way and not because I want to relegate you, but I give you these two scenarios because I think that could be the worst case and you were nowhere near that, but remember it could have been more than you think you inflected. I may have been mad for a brief moment but I think I can now thank you for your roll, because look at the way things have turned out to be for me, I would not have fled had it not be for the resentment I felt for all I know I would not have even made it to Aberdeen for such a mind moving experience on my part. Once again the word said give thanks for what ever situation you find yourself; I am very thankful for everything."

Neither man decided to suggest change of venue, as a result they stood right where they had exchange greetings and continue with the conversation in which they had both emerged themselves, each felt in their mind if it was comfortable with the other then why try to spoil a good thing, hence their conversation went on without being interrupted; each anticipating full awareness of the other in terms of the understanding of what is said.

They talked about everything including Pak's disappearance from home the controversy it sparked involving Sojy and the handsome inheritance at the center of it all to which Pak expressed his regret for the misunderstanding that occurred concerning him unapologetically a sentiment that was totally understandable to Sojy who in turned wish he could convince Pak to make one last visit back home to refute the situation which to some was still well alive, at his convenience to which Pak made no solid promise but welcomed the idea and wanted to know why Sojy was in Aberdeen, who was informed that they back home were in the process of carrying on some major developments and since Aberdeen was way ahead it was good to look at some of the good work that were already in play and make it a model of what is to come. With proper amends made by the two spent the rest of the time together catching up on all that happened since they last saw one another as they retrospect the days they had lived under the same roof. The following day the two met and said their good byes again with no promise of meeting any time soon but with a photography to bear witness to their encounter which Sojy could use as proof to those back home who would care to listen.

Just as he had disappeared in the dark of night, Pak resurfaced one bright morning in his birth place of Sankamaroo, and to those who knew him were so delighted that he really was alive and well at the same time making a positive impact on youths as well as adults, Sojy on the other hand was so delighted that Pak had made the journey back home to validate his innocence to Pak's disappearance and their encounter in the City of Aberdeen to which some were still doubtful. Pak who was met by his people to a rock star welcome only stayed two days and again he was gone just as he had arrived, not before promising Sojy that he would stay in touch but never to expect to see him again in Sankamaroo because of the memories imbedded in the town a decision quite understood by Sojy.

Chapter 6

With all the positive involvement in his community, when Pak came back to Aberdeen from his home town Sankamaroo, he came back far more focused then when he departed on the projects and activities that he was already involved in, it seems as though we went home and got reenergized, and with that renewed energy came a brand new vigor and enthusiasm, and as everyone who knew them would have imagined, his devoted and dedicated friend and support was there by his side to join forces with him to carry on their projects of interest, a move which made a lot of people to think, it was either a planned ordeal or they had both made the trip together since during his absence from Aberdeen she was only seen by less than five people in the community, and after his arrival they became almost inseparable except during school hours. One of the first and major Project Pak took on was the establishment of a youth newspaper between the City of Aberdeen and the Township of Sankamaroo where developmental ideas were constantly shared, with Sankamaroo being more of the beneficial party. Aberdeen also came out as the recipient of a rich cultural education that they knew little or nothing about. Adults as well as Children of Aberdeen could not believe that they were in the same Country with a slight difference in geographic location bearing a distance of just a little over two hundred miles had such a huge cultural diversity.

Since he was in his senior year in high school and had at least six to eight months before going off to college, Pak was not sure whether it would have been possible to accomplish the organization of an educational tour to the Township of Sankamaroo from Aberdeen through the authorities of the City of Aberdeen, considering the track record he had laid for himself through his many voluntary projects in the City of Aberdeen his success to see his dream come alive was so amazing he just could not believe the time it was achieved. Pak was particularly blown away when he personally received a communication from the Authorities of Sankamaroo, since in fact he had not had any formal meeting with them, during his short stay in his home town; But he made it his duty to acknowledge the manner in which the people and leaders of the Township of Sankamaroo preserved some of the Country's most valuable culture. A publication which sparked interest in the hearts and minds of the entire Nation, since it did receive National recognition thus promoting the writer of the article for his valuable contribution to the Nation, an important venture that paved the way for his future in the area of journalism, a profession which he had not really consider for the future. Pak became a prominent figure his last quarter in high school, he was no longer the kid who surfaced on the scene in the City of Aberdeen from nowhere, but was now a valuable resident of the great City, a City which was known not to be too welcoming to outsiders especially if they thought you were there to be assimilated in the advancement and development in regards to the City's well being. These were people that were so set in their way of life that they thought a change in any form, sounded so scary that whom ever it was, that was trying to mention said change was seen as an intruder who's trying to trample on the freedom of existence, and Pak this unknown homeless kid who had now grown into a fine and descent young man still in his teen had come to this local and served so well and sincere that even some of the most conservatives in the City, were willing to extend him an olive branch to the extent where others were ready to take him under their wings and provide him any necessary protection something that worked quite well in his favor, with all the trials and deaths he had gone through in his life, Pak was always a positive impact on any life he had encountered, and now that he was much more matured and taking on adult responsibilities, every thing he touched turned to gold. Again as optimistic as he was there were times when he faced bumps en route to some of his major undertakings, a feeling he often referred to as room for error, because as far as he was concerned, in life there is never ever a perfect situation, for that reason every time a beautiful dream came to his mind, his initial thought would include provision for set back even if there was a red carpet welcome written all over it, in view of that he always said to fail is to face life's reality, and once you've failed once, you will always get a better do over, remember, he would say it's not how many times one failed in life, it is how well one over came their failure and how well one can see the light at the end of the tunnel and convert it into an oasis of light from the distance which it was seen.

Pak's next move as always was another undertaking that even some of his very supporters thought was very much ambitious, he organize a youth event inviting the Authorities of both the Township of Sankamaroo and the City of Aberdeen, jointly awarding them for their valuable contributions and relentless efforts in all forms, an action that was highly anticipated by the audience and residents of both locals; what came as news to everyone else including those who had worked with him tirelessly, was; just when he was about to end his speech, he said; "Executives and Leaders of out two Locals, Ladies and Gentlemen here present for this all important occasion, as I retire to my seat I would like to take this time to establish a scholarship drive in honor of my two Mothers, for the benefit of under privilege children, and to this I would like to call it; The Ninuh Pehdus Scholarship Endowment and it will cater mainly to high school graduating seniors wishing to attain higher education, in universities or colleges of their choice as long as they are in good moral standing in their community and maintaining a two point zero grade point average." Before the audience could burst into cheers, he went on to say, "I beg you indulgence as I request a brief moment of silence for these two wonderful Women who have been the corner stone of my very existence," the next set of words that came out of his mouth immediately following the silence, were; "in gratitude for your congregation here this day and as Leaders of these two great Constituents in our beloved Nation, I ask that the City of Aberdeen make provision for a parcel of land to be used for the erection of a full fledge University offering under graduate degree for students of both locations including other surrounding, and as for the Township of Sankamaroo, we solicit your provision of labor to facilitate the advancement of this all important endeavor to cater to Townships and Cities, in this locality since in fact the nearest university is seven hundred and fifty miles away from the City of Aberdeen and nine hundred and fifty miles away from the Township of Sankamaroo." As if in response to his later request, the applaud from the audience was not only a loud one, but it came with a huge standing ovation, to that as Pak exited the stage shaking hands with the platform guest, his number one fan and admirer was right at the bottom of the stage's stairs patiently awaiting her turn to commend him for a job well done and to also deal him her dose of surprise as he had just done, only hers was not a well calculated, well kept secret packed speech in front of an elaborate audience that will yield a wave of applaud, which she was very pleased with any way because, as far as she was concerned this had been her well kept secret since the first time she laid eyes on Pak even though it was buried within her bosom for four years, it was well worth the wait. Pak stretched out both arms to his friend Suzette for a warm embrace and to apologize for not letting her in on the intricate parts of his just delivered still riding the wave of applaud in the background, her embrace was warm and firm to his body as well as the kiss she had planted across his lips with her tongue parting them and reaching to out his, Pak who never anticipated that in a million years was shocked and at a lost for words after his first kiss that lasted for at least three seconds but felt like eternity, when he finally broke away from the kiss their embrace was still in tact their gaze locked in, and it must have been another seven seconds before he was able to recollect his thoughts and say something to his dear Friend and Partner, in his usual soft and firm voice, he said "what was that all about?" with her not wasting any moment to answer, she said; I have been waiting for a long time to do this and I just didn't know how you were going to take it, and tonight for considering that you will only be here for another twelve weeks before you depart for college and I'm not sure I want you to leave without knowing what I feel for you inside and inform you how long has this vessel of flesh and blood of mine been harboring it all inside. I also want you to know that if this is something that you wish not to pursue, I will totally understand with no reservation of mine in me whatsoever in as much as I would prefer the affirmation for my action toward you this evening and if things don't go my way, I still hope that we continue to work together as we have been doing in the past." This time before Pak could say another word, Suzette once again had her arms around his neck and her tongue fumbling his mount for his, Pak went along as if it was an act planned and was being executed by the pair. This time when they broke from one another's embrace, Pak said; "if that's how you feel, I am unopposed to your wishes, but I don't know why you had to wait this long, as you said yourself, I'm here for twelve more weeks and I'll be traveling seven hundred and fifty miles for school and there is no telling how often I'll be able to make it back here to see you during school breaks, and it's not like I will be having them every week, we would have spent a lot of time together leading up to this moment my only hope is that what ever it is that we are doing, is the right thing." The encounter with Suzette, lasted about a minute and the half, just as they were in the process of breaking their embrace, the voice of Father John Georges rang in the ears of Pak; "you've made me a very proud man Pak," the spiritual leader was saying, as he approached them. I also want to inform you that I'm not the only one who's walking on clouds now because of what you just did out there, there's a whole lot of people out there who will be waiting in line to commend you for such a brilliant venture that you've undertaken since you made an appearance on the scene in this City, and now that you've extended your generosity to the Township of Sankamaroo, the scope has broaden, you need to prepare your hand for the amount of hand shakes you are about to receive, and while you were at it, make some time available, because it will be a long line, but it's all in good faith, you are the man who has done his home work quite well, I wish you all the best because now you're a leader and you'll need all the luck, blessings and guidance that you will need in this path in life that you've decided to travel." The priest concluded, even though Pak at the time, had not pay much attention to what Father Georges was saying, he kept at the back of his mind, because that's the kind of individual Pak was, he would never miss an opportunity to absorb a good lesson, even if it was just sporadic statement made on a casual basis, because as he had learned earlier on in life on one of the brief moments spent with his biological Father,; every good lesson acquired and banked, could end up being vey useful some day some where down the line on ones journey in life.

Just as Father John Georges had advice Pak earlier, immediately after his speech, as he walked into the adjoining room from where the program was held, the very leaders that he had addressed directly were all waiting to meet and commend him on his achievement thus far and register their support for the request he had made. The evening turned out to be one of the best soiree in his life because it elevated him to a different level on the leadership scene, and also on this particular day, his path to leadership was paved even though he did no know it then considering he was still a graduating senior who was already a college prospect seven hundred and fifty miles away.

After that memorable program with the City and Township Leaders, and with barely two months to leave for college, Pak seemed to have been every where every week which was a very good timing since he was on vacation from school, and he was addressing various youth programs and at the same time confabulating with the Authorities of not Just the Township of Sankamaroo and the City of Aberdeen, but other cities and towns in between, sleeping only two nights a week in his studio apartment on a single styled bed, even though he enjoyed the trips and V.I.P. treatments that were offered him free of charge they were not really free, because he was busy giving advice and restructure a lot of these groups, which he did not mind doing, but it always felt good when he was at home in his own bed, because those were the moments he spent with his new love and best Friend Suzette, who had also his principal deputy on most if not all of the projects he under took, but only traveled once on these many trips he had made, who then concluded that the trips were very tedious and intense and that her being around was simply a distraction for him, since she was only able to share a little or far less time with him and at the end of the day when it was time to relax, he was so tired all he would do was go straight to sleep and get some rest to muster enough strength for the next day, and they spent three days together in all on that particular trip which turned out to be more than enough for her. After those energy draining days, Pak had to himself a clear schedule for the last week before his departure to school, to allow him enough time to prepare for the up coming school which definitely a new territory that might produce some new encounters to life and he needed to clear his head before venturing onto this unfamiliar terrain. Pak who continued working with the youth organizations and authorities of the City of Aberdeen, made sure that this time his Love and best Friend Suzette was always with him during these last days before his departure, not just for the purpose of their romantic relationship, but there was a huge benefit in it also for their professional relationship and she being his principal deputy and a co partner on most if not all of these projects her presence was very vital because after he leaves, she will be the one in charge and needed all the necessary information to pick up where he left off, at the same time with all the last minute finishing touches Suzette on the other had her own secret mission for him, and that mission was to send him off in grand style the Friday before his departure for school, an event that she had been planning since she came back from the one and only trip she had accompanied him on when he was going through that tedious and tiring voyage that entailed a never ending energy. Suzette impressed on her parent to be the ones handling the elite and Business Community of the City of Aberdeen and some of the Authorities and Youth Leaders from his home town of Sankamaroo with emphasis on Sojy's presence and other cities and townships he had recently visited, even though his voyage was intense, he never during his tour made it back to Sankamaroo, not that he really cared, but that idea never surfaced and he on his part did not make any mention in that regard so he thought the next time he's back in town on vacation from school, he will make it his business to revisit his home town of Sankamaroo, but now he will deal what's in his immediate reach, because as he thought, it will only boost his moral while he was away in school and people will have something to remember him by, because this City means a lot to him, if anything, it helped shaped and mould his path in life as conservative as it had been anticipated to be, and all that was made possible because of Father John Georges arm of solidarity extended to him.

The send off for Pak turned out to be such a huge event, it was beyond the imagination of the main organizer Suzette, it turned out that she herself never got to know the exact location for the event until the day before, her parents and the City Mayor when introduced to the idea of a send off for Pak and considering the many contributions he had made in the last three years out of the four that he had become a resident of the City of Aberdeen, would go a long way in thanking him for his positive attributes to youths and adults and the many lives he touched so for him the City's National Ballroom will serve very well in that light, above all they vigorously emerged themselves with the responsibility of making sure the out of town high powered guest and the prominent individual residing in land were reminded that this is not just a send off party but also an occasion of recognition from a young and upcoming Leader in the Nation's History, especially when they had to retrospect that historic event spear headed by him that gave birth to that higher educational unification complex speech that earned him a standing ovation, and an entrance to the leadership platform which to a certain degree he was now riding on.

Suzette did not get too excited until she found out the location where the event was to be held, because most time when an event that huge was to be held in town people would start arriving by mid week, but as she had pleaded with her parents to keep it top secret until the time arrived they went on to caution their out of town guest mostly to start arriving on the morning of the send off. A heed that was well taken by all involved.

On the morning of the send off for Pak, Suzette woke up early with something very intriguing on her mind aside from the big event for her Lover and Best Friend, and that was she really would have a minute or two with Sojy whom she would love to talk to about what kind of person Pak was growing up, since he was the only known family alive for Pak that they all knew, and base on discussions that she had been having with Pak after his visit to Sankamaroo it just might warm his heart to know that someone from his place of birth or better yet a family member would be in attendance, she was so amaze and hype about the thought that was circling on her mind until

She was told by her parents that Sojy would not be in attendance and will not make the trip to the City of Aberdeen for the send off and recognition of Pak a news which crushed her zeal and moral, as hard as it was for her, she had to put herself together and get ready for the event of the evening.

For Pak it was a normal Friday, and all he knew was there was an event hosted by the Mayor of the City of Aberdeen for the various youth program and to encourage them to keep doing the good deeds they were already involved in and to remain grounded now that one of their own was about to go away for school makes it all worth the cause because they could follow in his footsteps and make their City more accommodating for future endeavors, on that note every meeting that he attended his message was to let the participants know that even though he will be seven hundred and fifty miles away he will always be along side them in all their undertakings, plus he would make it his business to be back every chance he gets even if it was for a week or two, and that the line of communication to him was wide open between him and all organizations that felt a need for his views and input on any matter pertinent to them, and that he will forever be a part of them, a message which was not taken lightly by those who had closely worked with him, because they were the ones who knew his level of commitment and dedication to projects he aligned himself with, and now that he was about to leave them in charge they would make sure that all that they had planned will and must be executed in case he came back he would be able to see his brain child alive and highly operational.

Pak wrapped up his day around three fifteen that afternoon, in order to go home relax and get ready for the program of the evening, because in his mind he just knew in as much as he was not in the fore front of what was taking place that evening, due to his involvement with the various youth programs and activities he would be called upon at least once to say something before the evening is over so he may as well be prepared and well rested before the hour is here. He did not pen down anything formal, since he was an extemporaneous speaker base on what the event was geared toward for that evening, he would just speak in connection with the theme of the day, which of course he would learn upon his arrival at the occasion that evening.

Just before he could enter the compound that has been his home for the last four years as a resident of the City of Aberdeen, Father John Georges called out to him from across the street, when he turned around to look in the direction where the man who had been his Spiritual Guidance and Father since the very first day he landed in the City was standing with Suzette and someone he knew he had seen before but could not remember when and where, but he was not going to loose any sleep over the thought of what was going through his mind after all he had visited at least a thousand locations in the last nine weeks and he won't be able to remember ever detail and every person of the tour he had just finished. He was about to walk in the direction toward the trio when Father Georges motioned him to stay put because they were advancing toward him. The three were barely two yards from Pak when he recognized who exactly it was that was walking with Father Georges and Suzette, he called out the name "Chotas, is that you?" Inquired Pak, "I didn't think you would remember me, because the last time you saw me it was for less than fifteen minutes, and before then you were too young to remember at least that's how I felt" replied Chotas.

Chotas is Sojy's eldest son from his first marriage, the one that he really never got over even while he was married to Ninuh before she died, there were repeated friction in respect to that some of which the then little Pak had to be a recipient from Sojy who was not so fond of him as he was considered more of a rival than a step son, all because according to him "Sojy" his ex-wife had turned the kids against him as a result he had no domain of discipline over his own kids, which led to them turning out to be a burden in society a feeling that made him powerless because he had no control over it until things got completely out of hands, but to Pak's surprise when he made the trip back to Sankamaroo, Chotas had turned his life around and was doing some good things in the community an information which came through to Pak in the form of a gossip. But when the two finally met, and because of their schedule they did not have time to talk and Pak left town before Chotas could get some time to schedule another meeting. Chotas who after hearing that Pak was going to be leaving town and going even further away from them, and after seeing some in Sankamaroo and hearing of the so many contributions and achievements associated with Pak was doing every thing to be a part of the recognition ceremony in honor of Pak even though he knew it was a surprise to Pak and Sojy had no concrete reason for staying away he would be the one from Sankamaroo representing the family for a native of the Township of Sankamaroo, because for him, it was about giving a man his flowers while he's alive and this young gentleman had earned every branch that awaited him at that recognition program later on, it was his day and it had to be all about him and no one else, Sojy his Father had missed one of the most important days in his life and it was his lost.

A surprised Pak extended his hand for a shake as Chotas was in arms length saying; you and your Daddy sure do know how to make surprise visits to this City, how is everyone else doing? And what brings you to town?" He asked Chotas. Chotas jokingly replied saying; I heard that you were about to leave the City of Aberdeen to a far away land, and since you my brother from the Township of Sankamaroo have made such a huge impact during your stay here I wanted to come and with your blessing replace you, I would have done so earlier but this City is not big enough for two Natives from the Township of Sankamaroo, considering the huge difference you've made so I had to wait because our presence must always be felt, and I'm here to do just that and as soon as you return from you discovery I'll be waiting right here to remit the fruit of your labor back to your care. Pak who was amuse as everyone else in hearing distance in a flattered voice responded,

"I'm glad that the Township of Sankamaroo is alive and eager to replace and dedicate it's Natives for such positive cause so that mankind can continue to prosper and impact positive attitudes to the weakest link on the chain of human development." Father John Georges joined in and said Fellows remember that without the permission and cooperation of the residents of this great City none of you will be able to find your way anywhere in this City." Then now it was time for Suzette to add her voice to the conversation, "Gentlemen I must remind you that if the Natives of the Great City of Aberdeen was not as welcoming and friendly as we were brought up based on our cultural and humanitarian values, none of you would have felt the need to even stop or stay over night in this City, let alone getting assimilated, you must all remember that you're forever indebted to us for our generosity and kindness."

To that statement the guys giggle and one at a time declined to respond directly, because it was a common knowledge then that you don't argue with a lady no matter how young or old, but if you over looked the myth went ahead with the argument ninety nine percent of the time you would loose and if you did you would end up loosing ninety nine argument before you could ever win another one, so they each jokingly said the lady has spoken and laughed about it.

"There is an event going on tonight at the City Hall Ballroom if you stay over night you should come I'm expected to be there and since you are a guest from Sankamaroo and most of the youth groups from around the City will also be in attendance, there are things you could take back home for the work that you do also Chotas" Pak said addressing his Townsman.

"That's very kind Pak, coming from you it means a whole lot to me now I really which my Dad and other Siblings were here to share in this all important occasion," trying very hard not to give away any part of the surprise that was to unfold during the event of the evening, and I promise in all sincerity I will never miss this for all the money in this World thanks a million for inviting me, what time does it start?" Chotas asked "It starts at eight thirty, but unlike the Township of Sankamaroo in this City the doors officially open an hour before the start time of any planned event and guest are being received immediately thereafter, and we the youth organizations of this City have done very well to keep that particular pattern enforced, and the reason why that is done is to give people ample time to meet greet mix and mingle before the main event, that way people don't spend quality time from the program to do that, and once the program starts, it's the only thing you're occupied with. Where are you stopping?" Pak concluded.

I will be there and on time, I'm checked in at the Pussy Cat Motel a block from the City Hall so that makes it very easy to be on time and because of you and the briefing that I've just received, I won't be late for all the treasures this World has to offer, that said I have a very dear request, I want you to promise me this time on a much serious note that you won't leave town without seeing me, cause I think you and me got some talking to do." Chotas replied.

I sincerely promise that I will not leave town without telling you and to add on to that I think it will be a good thing for you and I to have a talk before I leave but it all depends on how long you're in town for, because I leave by next Thursday about a week from today and after today, I will have a very light load of business on my plate until Wednesday which is the eve of my departure where I might get entrenched in some last minute frustrating hassle just for the fun of it that's my schedule so you can pick a slot and fit me in."

"What's about three fifteen tomorrow afternoon in the lobby of the Pussy Cat Motel where I'm staying currently?" Chotas inquired.

"Three fifteen at the Pussy Cat Motel it is my good Brother."

After the dialogue between Pak Chotas the Priest, the conversation spotlighted again on Suzette who this time wanted to know from the three men if they had time to eat and really relax before the evening ahead, because as she put it you men will spend all the time doing anything unrelated to what is ahead, and with just a limited time to play with you'll end up power rushing your preparation thereby tending to compact activity in ratio to time. This time around the three men with one accord agreed that, that's where the difference between a male and a profuse female and that a male doesn't need as much time as a female to get dressed for an event, and when it comes to feeding, just like shopping a male knows how hungry he is, he sets his mind on and what's available to feed on then makes his move by advancing on the most appealing, so in short the answer to her concern by acclamation of the three was that they had enough time to accomplish what needed to be before the unfolding hour of the event for the evening.

As if on a rehearsed schedule by the three men, they arrived simultaneously at the City Hall Ball Room Entrance at exactly seven thirty three and were all escorted to the second row of seats from the stage in the building's main auditorium where a formal recognition program was to be held in honor of Pak who still had no idea what it was about, and to keep him deep in the darkness per Suzette's request, she had asked that at this program there be no platform guest, because that would mean giving Pak a seat on the podium and she did not want him to have the least suspicion before his name was called and the reason mentioned, as we've already come to know, Suzette is the kind of individual who can keep and conceal a secret like she did with her crush on Pak.

By eight fifteen the auditorium was full to capacity with even the standing room being well occupied, which led the rest of the guest no access to the auditorium, they had to wait for the formal program to be over and they can all go into the Ballroom together for the festive part of the program, it turned out even those who were in the fore front for the organization of the event underestimated the work and contribution made by Pak, worst of all they did not expect that a lot of people would have wanted to be a part of an event in his honor especially when they learn that he will be going away for at least four years, everyone wanted to show their respect for this remarkable young man who has made a lot of difference with if not all, almost all youth groups in the region not just in the City of Aberdeen. So, at age sixteen and a college freshman, they felt it a need to elevate him in a way where no matter where he ends up he will always see them as a part of his every undertaking. For this and other reasons when the name came up for recognition everyone was willing to join the band wagon. The secret was pretty safe until four minutes before the start of the program, a lady from a nearby city who had never met Pak but had heard a lot about him, She was sitting directly behind the seat of Chotas who was sitting next to Pak on the left said, I really would like to meet this young man named Pak, he must be very remarkable for all these people to assemble here today just to honor him, he must have a very proud set of parents boosting of him and all that he has accomplished at such a young of sixteen, he is a force to reckon with which we had more young people like him in this World. Pak turned his head slightly on the left to see who it was, and realize that he did not know this lady and could not remember ever meeting her, but then he realized that Father John Georges and Chotas were looking at the lady as if to say don't you know you are not suppose to say what you just said, but they both knew now that it was already too late and the cat was out of the bag due to some talkative lady from God knows where.

Chapter 7

Chotas journey to the great City of Aberdeen was highly unanticipated, one thing was sure was the way he felt about his Father Sojy whom he hadn't really had a cordial relationship with and as he grew much older and started getting involved with projects in the Township of Sankamaroo, he was even more disgusted with some of the evil things he learned his Father was associated with, but due to cultural upbringing and measures instituted by the local teachings of the Township he wouldn't dare confront his Father "Sojy" in any way shape or form, as a result, when the news came that there was a program planned to recognize the many contributions of Pak who was a Native of the Township of Sankamaroo, and the people of the City of Aberdeen would prefer an official representation from the Township of Sankamaroo along with a chosen family member, and since he Sojy was already familiar with the area and had already been introduced to the conspiracy which was in progress, would be the perfect candidate for said mission. His very first question to the suggestion, was, what's in it for him? Sounds just like you Sojy! If there was no gain in it for him he has no interest. Chotas who had just walked in on the conversation to hear his Father say to the individuals bearing the message that; "the boy is not my son I don't even care if he turns out to be a good for nothing human being, it wouldn't border me and his achievement in life is of no importance to me, and the reason why I went to The City of Aberdeen in the first place, was I wanted to see for my self that he was alive and convince him to come back for everyone else to have a visual of him and then I can collect what was rightfully mine, and it turned out I did not have to do a whole lot of talking, because all I did, was pretended like I was sorry for what I did and he bought the whole story, which led to him coming back here, and that was even sooner than I thought which gives me the impression that I must have done a pretty darn good job on him.

As you already know I did not have to spend any money of my own, my entire trip was financed by the fools in the City of Aberdeen who thought they had found themselves a golden child and to make sure that no one else would come after him, to tell you the truth, if I had my way he would have perished with Ninuh when she died, because he was still alive that's why it took me so long to claim the inheritance, and to make a bad matter worst, the little fool took his ass out of town in he middle of the night leaving a bulk of the people here to think that I had done something to him, the fact of the matter is, I didn't have to do anything to his stupid ass and I was still going to get that wealth." When Chotas over heard this, he was deeply troubled and wanted to do everything in his power to make his Father pay for such wicked deed, but really didn't know how to go about it, but he had to act and act fast, because time was not on his side, just when he thought he was about to run out of options, that's when it hit him, and then he moved into the center of the room where the discussion was being held at which time he was clearly visible by every one present which were his Father and the Chief Executive of the Township of Sankamaroo, with both men gaze fixed on him, he greeted and offered to make the trip to City of Aberdeen as he insinuated that it could even be a good time for him to also pay a visit to the great City which was also in the process of establishing a bilateral relationship with the Township of Sankamaroo, he further lamented that it was a gesture that could help their cause and foster a better working rapport between the youths of the two locations, which made a lot of sense to the Town's Official who with out any hesitation accepted the offer whole heartedly, and told Chotas that it was an all expense paid trip and all he had to do was show up and be ready to travel.

Chotas who had only heard part of the conversation, wanted to know if he had to prepare a speech for the occasion or if they would rather have him say what they wanted, and if so who will be putting it together. The Elderly State Man once again impressed on him to do as he pleased since as he put it, it was a youth thing and they better knew the kind of language that was most appropriate for the occasion, as long as it was cordial in it's contents it was good enough for the Township of Sankamaroo, reminding him that the current government was only in power for a short time and pretty soon the youth will be in charge of the leadership of their respective locations and this was a good time to start practicing, all of which was well taken and highly digested. In as much as he was delighted that it was all a brilliant idea, his primary goal was to see how he could meet with Pak and see how best he could muster the ability to present what had just transpired between his Father and the Town's executive that he walked in on, because his Father Sojy abruptly left town one day to the City of Aberdeen almost penniless spent about a week and ten days after he got back he was flying high with a lot of money shortly after Pak came to town, spending less than three days then disappearing and now here he is walking in on an evil conversation between his Father and this Man who's considered one of the most powerful, if not the most in the Township of Sankamaroo. At the end of the day Chotas was very delighted that he was making the trip and he would do the best to get all he anticipants out of such remarkable and historical trip which beside his intention to uncover any evil deeds that his Father was involved might end up being a fruitful and rewarding adventure.

Chotas who up until the day he was expected to leave knew that he was the only one making the trip to The City of Aberdeen was shock to learn two days before his departure, that his Father "Sojy" would like to make the trip with him for fear that he might get lost since the City of Aberdeen was eight times the size of the Township of Sankamaroo, and that in order for him to go they would both have to foot some of the traveling expenses, which included but not limited to ticket, food, and lodging, when he heard those words from Sojy's mouth, he looked at him as if he had just seen a ghost or an alien from outer space, he struggle hard to contain himself from being rude to his

Father, all he did, since he still had a little more time was find his way to the Town's Council to find the man who had accepted the offer after Sojy first refused, to find out if it was his idea that the two of them should make the trip under the stipulated conditions. The Council Man then explain to Chotas that, Sojy had been trying to be a part of the trip since he accepted the offer, and had suggested that they both foot some of the cost of the trip, at which time he said, he then told Sojy that the ball was in Chotas court and if that was something that he wanted to do then he could go ahead he had nothing to do with it, because when he Sojy was first confronted he flat out refused, when Chotas learned of that he went back to Sojy and told him that they would definitely make the trip together, and since they had a day or say or so left, he would meet with him the day before the trip for the two to go down to the bus station and make the necessary arrangement to get every thing in motion, a proposal that was welcomed and accepted by Sojy.

Chotas was very happy with the acceptance on the part of Sojy who did not think anything out of the ordinary about his Son's proposal, little did he know that he would not be making the trip with Chotas, and if he insisted on going they would have to travel separately. Chotas then went directly to the bus station and made an arrangement which he had to pay extra for to be picked up on the out sketch of the town so his seat wouldn't be taken by someone else at the bus station, and he gave himself two hours before the time to meet with Sojy he left center town to the area where he would catch the bus. He was so secretive with plans that less than five persons were aware including he and the Councilman who were concern with the circumstance surrounding the trip, fortunately for Chotas everything went as planned, a decision that he was very pleased with, because it was either that or have to face his Father with some disgusting words which he knew was not in his best interest considering cultural depiction with regards to their tradition, so his action was more than appropriate for the situation at hand.

Chotas was picked up by the bus on the schedule date and time while his Father Sojy canvas the Center of the Township of Sankamaroo looking for Chotas, who at first thought his son had decided to bail out because he was afraid of making the trip based on what he had learned about the City of Aberdeen until he got down to the bus station a day after the trip to be told that Chotas had made the trip, he had arranged to be picked up at the edge of town, and as far as they knew everything went as planned.

Chotas ride to the great City of Aberdeen was smooth as it was exciting, upon arrival he was not prepare for the sight that he was face with, no one had told him that this was such a beautiful place, but that aside, in as much as his Father Sojy had tried to warn him in advance about the size it was an as he could see under statement and people were everywhere, the best part of it all was that the entire thing had been planned in advance he was only to wait and see where it would all go.

Suzette was at the Aberdeen National Terminal on time to meet Sojy and who ever was accompanying him to the recognition program planned for Pak she wasn't too sure if she would have recognized him since she had only seen him once, for that reason she hoped he would be carrying a sign marked D-San indicating that it was the delegation from Sankamaroo. It only made sense because that's what she was told the day before when she was informed by her Father that she would have to be the one meeting the group from Sankamaroo without mentioning to her in particular who it was, but based on her knowledge and persistent to have someone from that region present for the event, with emphasis on Sojy, she assumed that it was none other than Sojy being accompanied by a youth leader, after all she had no reason to believe any thing unforeseen, because she was made to believe that he had come out on good faith and was willing to travel more than two hundred miles just to come and make amends with Pak whom he had so deeply scared as a child who later on decided to flee from home because he did not want this man who had a negative effect on his life to continue being a part of his childhood, so he took the best way he knew how.

She finally saw the marked sign but did not recognize the individual carry it, and she also noticed that the sign was being accompanied by a single person and not two as she had anticipated, with mixed emotions she advanced in the direction of the sign, her first question was geared toward throwing some light on the where about of Sojy and a knowledge of what happened to the second delegate since the City of Aberdeen was expecting at least two visitors, when confronted by Suzette, Chotas who at the time did not want to go into any details, simply implied he had to make the trip alone because of a last minute emergency just about the time their trip was schedule, and he being the most prominent youth leader in the Township had to design a strategy and come up with a plan to make sure their Township was fully represented considering the gravity stressed in the communication received with regards to the importance of the event which involved a Native from the Township of Sankamaroo.

Chotas who was in his second day in the City of Aberdeen after spending the first night in the hotel he was staying was so amuse by the size of the City of Aberdeen and the population therein that he could not contain his emotions, as he repeatedly expressed them to Suzette who was not too surprised based on what she had learned earlier from Pak who had expressed to her that anyone entering the City of Aberdeen for the first time from his home town of Sankamaroo will forever be fascinated by the ambience in the City, because they were used to smaller locations a far few human population and when it comes to the City of Aberdeen, the Township of Sankamaroo is child's play thus prompting the excitement, amusement and concern in his voice and attitude, especially when he said; "behold the City where the entire World intersects." Even Suzette could not help but produce a broad smile which turned into a grain, I like this guy already she thought to her herself not really transcribing it into words. Chotas was having such a ball with his sight seeing he did not notice Father John Georges when he approached and greeted him and Suzette, he only came down to reality when Suzette tapped him on the shoulder while he was introducing him to the man of God who as Chotas realize had his hand stretched out for a hand shake indicating the sincerity of the introduction, extending his hand Chotas expressed his gratitude to the Catholic priest for their combine effort to include the Township of Sankamaroo in the event recognizing one of their own, whom they all have had tremendous regards for because of his contribution to society, he further declared to both Suzette and Father Georges that the entire Township of Sankamaroo was highly gratified just to know that a City as great as Aberdeen could afford to give them a seat at the table for such historic occasion means a lot to them, and it signifies that the little Township is also capable of making an impact on life's great stage when given the chance to, and not only have they shine the light of the strength and power of combined efforts, but have also shown that the world continues to appear to foster the pavement of the road which transforms it into becoming a Global village when people collectively work together for the enhancement of human development in every aspect in life. With all that he was saying to these two he could not wait to finally meet with Pak who in the first place was the reason that motivated him to make this historic journey, he also for a minute thought, he had a whole lot to discuss with Pak who had made such a huge difference in life to the extend where he was now bringing two groups of people together for a common goal which will survive decades if not centuries beyond his own days on this earth.

Father Georges who had been patiently listening to this excited stranger, with no offer of any help in the capacity which he was speaking , couldn't help but reflect back on his first encounter with the then young Pak who had been so full of life excitement and hope for his newly found home even though he was in a hopeless situation, his demeanor in terms of how he interacted with others did not seem to absorb the negative aspect of the ocean he was in, instead it portrayed an enthusiastic individual who was willing to meet life's challenges with every fighting bone in his body and overcome obstacles yet to face. A major quality that caused Father John Georges to be more enticed to render the young man every assistant he possibly could, thus leading to this particular moment a, realization which brought joy to his inner soul, he could not help but think to himself that of all the thirteen years that he had spent in the Catholic Priest hood this in the last three had been the most fruitful and rewarding, which started since the first time he laid eyes on Pak and as the thought linger in his mind, he also could not help but imagine that the trend of success attributed to Pak will never be completed without him being mentioned, as selfish as it sounded, he knew that was really the truth, and there was no if's ands and buts about it. Father Georges who after playing the entire episode in his mind and digesting every word that created an echo on his ear drum, reassured Chotas that as long as the world continues to evolve mankind will forever remain one another's support for the development of a peaceful tomorrow and a planet free of warfare, greed, anger deceit but as he rightly put it, it will take the contribution of every level headed and sound minded individual alive to make the sacrifice in the most humanly accepted moral fashion, and that Pak had achieved that which off course makes him a prime example of what a lot of us should be doing in this day and time.

Chotas for his part expressed his gratitude and appreciation once again to Father Georges for being the force and voice of reasoning who at the time to even acknowledge the potential of a person he did not know or had never had any previous encounter with, a gesture on his part which has paved the path to build the platform for the stage that they currently find themselves, concluding that, he Father Georges is truly a caring and dedicated humanitarian first and foremost but above, the God that he worships really is the one and only Almighty and Living God who is no respecter of class possessions or status due to the manner in which he accepted Pak into his heart and confidence. Chotas finally inquired; has Pak been informed about my arrival?" Suzette quickly replied, I don't think Pak has the slightest idea that you or anyone from your Township would be attending this event, to answer your question, as far as I'm concern he doesn't, well except where maybe Father Georges told him, but it was all meant to be a surprise and I think the residents in this City know how to keep a surprise alive and well."

Just as she was ending her phrase, Father John Georges cut in, "I think I've been in this City long enough to know what the City requires when it comes to making people feel special even if it is a surprise, now Suzette you know I wouldn't want to be the one to spoil your good moment, for that reason since the day I received the communication that this was going to be a surprise I made it my business to seal my lips until the moment to let the cat out of the bag. Chotas lamented to the two that, he was happy to be a part of the event at hand even if it meant he be a part of the secret, which for him was a thing that would be appreciated by most."

They were in the middle of the discussion when Father John Georges looked up and saw Pak, thereby informing them that Pak was about to make an entrance into the compound where he lived which was just across the street from where they were, that was when Father Georges called out the name of Pak, as the walked in his direction with the intention of reuniting him with a native of the township of Sankamaroo, they met and chatted for a brief moment after which they all planned to meet later at the entrance of the venue where the event was to be held that evening.

Pak who until he was called upon to the stage even after the talkative lady let out the surprise right next to him, still seemed not to have had any idea of what the main attraction of the event was, ascended the stage highly emotional, a side of him that a lot of people were seeing for the first time when he was made aware that he was the reason for the event and that without him everyone from these different geographic locations would not have been present in the City of Aberdeen given that from the day he made it on the scene of the development of human resource to his community he had taken on a new role, even his Mentor and surrogate Father, had never seen the part of Pak on the stage that evening, which also caused his eyes to water as well. Pak after being recognized at the event and all present, was also able to pull himself together and deliver an extemporaneous speech with so much power which touched every single individual present at the event. In his speech as highlighted he admonished the adults to bring up the youth in a loving and dedicated fashion, for as he put it the responsibilities of a civilized society anticipated by decent people of the world, is carved by it's elders which were the youth of yesterday, and as they exit the scene for future generation, the road paved by them must not only be that which was received from their forefathers, but it should be in a much more advanced and improved state, because since the beginning of time, the world evolves on a daily basis, and to the youths he informed them that the world will not remember us for the good life we live the days we spent on this earth, rather it will remember us for the contribution made to our fellow man that touches one's life in the manner in which it caused a ripple effect which trickles down the line in time, so when ever history is written, that particular difference will forever be mentioned. At the end of his oration he was elevated by the audience to a standing ovation which lasted at least fifteen seconds which appeared at the time to be eternity, but it was well worth it considering the contribution made thus far by this brilliant young mind who by a long shot has not really started to experience his own potential as it relates to the human race.

After the oration, Pak descended the stage to the standing ovation of all at the event, most importantly to the encouragement, acknowledgement, approval and the embrace of his most trusted allies present, namely; Father John Georges, Suzette and of course Chotas, who was most recently added to the bunch since his arrival in the City of Aberdeen and his meeting with Pak.

When the honoring ceremony for Pak was over he realized then that he had come a long way, and just as he had made up his mind then to leave the township of Sankamaroo for an adventure to a strange land once again it was time to make another move, just this time he won't have to sneak in the back of a pickup truck, rather he's been sent away with honors and respect for a greater achievement in yet another strange land, a thought which made him to retrospect what his biological Father once told him during one of their brief sections together, he said; "as a man never get over comfortable with your surrounding, for you don't know when you might be abruptly interrupted to leave your comfort zone for an unknown destination, and also learn to adjust because you never know how long you could be placed in an unfamiliar territory, some times for your own good or for the worst reason possible," he also went on to say that; "not every anticipated good situation is good for everyone, and the thought that there is always greener grass on the other side, what is not being said, is that you have to get on the other side and find out that the grass has to be developed and nurtured by you for others to comment on the vision of it's rich green color and carpet formation over the earth which it occupied." His thought was interrupted by his lover and number one Fan Suzette who was giving him a message from her Father who wanted Pak to make sure to get in touch with him before his departure for the journey of his life long adventure, as he jokingly put it. Pak who had been spending most of his time with Suzette for the past several months and weeks knew deep down inside that he would miss her dearly, since in fact, he had not made a move yet and he was missing her already, he also knew that if he wanted to make the best of life he had to acquire all the knowledge and education he could get his hands on, and for him, the sky was the limit and in order to achieve that he must do what is required, for he anticipated they had more time in the not too distant future to spend eternity together, but right now first things first, and when they finally get back together they would pick up from where the left off, and besides he would be visiting every possible chance he gets, and they would spend their holidays together and it will only be two years when they will once again be reunited, in the main time the reason why Pak was asked to get in touch with Suzette's Father, was for an offer which will afford him a steak in his bakery business which happens to be the most lucrative in the entire City of Aberdeen, not just as an employee, but a partner, if it was something he wanted but this was just to let him know that if he ever needed a job, he already had one as an in coming college freshman who had not even had his first college classroom experience, once again as always Pak was humbled and gracious for the offer and accepted with a rain check, not without pledging that if that's the will of the Lord it will all come to pass, since he's the one who makes everything that is possible, possible!

Chotas who had not really had a real one on one talk with Pak as he had anticipated wanted to make sure that he gets his exclusive moment with Pak since he did not know when they would have another opportunity to be once again reunited, and there was so much that he wanted to say to Pak that was for his own good and safety, but when he finally got the chance to his moment with Pak and considering the joy and happiness the event of the evening had poured on him, he did not want to spoil the day for him and he was also very delighted to be a part of the entire ordeal. All he could say to Pak, was; he had made a great leader and a designed role model out of himself, and that his future was so bright that it could spark a huge flame from the distance, he also beg him not to forget his home town of Sankamaroo, for they don't only admire his bold and influential character, but through him, Sankamaroo could be a part of the major leagues as it relates to social and geopolitics on the national and global stage, for as he puts it, he sees Pak going places and doing big things not just to his own glory but to the edification of those most deserving, not forgetting to assign credit where it is due and encouragement where it is required the most, an observation by Chotas when revealed to Pak made him once again to relive a conversation with his biological Father who once told him that; "in life one must always strive to be oneself, and that whatever it is that one tries to do make sure it's done to the best of ones ability, and never be afraid to fail because failure is a part of life which informs you that there is never always a smooth road to success, failure only serves as a stumbling block, saying go back and look over what you have done so far, just in case you forget to cross a "T" or dot an "I" because you control your own destiny in this life guided by the Divine Hands of God Almighty, bear in mind for as long as you live, that; a determine is never perturbed." It was at this juncture that Pak finally came to realize that even though he had not spend a great deal of time with his bio Father, he learned a lot from him during those brief moments to the extend that the lessons learned is showing up in his life and he was able to retain them where lately he can even make reference to them an amazing thought which made him to say out loud "thank you Father." As the words came out of his mouth and landed on the ear drum of Father John Georges who was in ear shot and thought then that he was being addressed by Pak, express his gratitude once again to Pak, and reiterated how proud a man Pak had made him since he crossed path with the once hopeful young child who at an early age in his life knew exactly what he wanted to do with his life and has not once lost track of what he set off to do then, and that it's all visible in the life that he leads four plus years after their first encounter.

Pak felt so good and overwhelm by all the love and attention he was receiving on this God given day, a feeling which had him turning the events of his early life over in his mind constantly when it hit him, he wish his Mother, Ninuh and his Father were all alive to see what had become of their one time little boy who by their constant memory has continue to break down barriers, and by their profound spiritual guidance has also continue to excel in ways he never thought possible, and by their example he has been able to reciprocate love for hate and peace and calm for hostility. In his mind, he felt very blessed and said to him self, that the world in which we live is more generous and kind than most people can ever imagine we are only consume with the few evil taking place, because we take the good things for granted.

Pak was planning to make the best out of the few more hours he had to spend with everybody around him because as far as he was concerned this is the family that he has and will always remember, and was willing to do what ever he could in his weak way to let them know how much he appreciates and adore their presence and involvement in his life, and this for him will forever be home. He spent the rest of the night meeting and getting acquainted with people he had not met and greeting and thanking those who were able to make it to attend the milestone event. When the meet and greet section was over it was almost midnight, at which time a select group was invited to a gathering of about forty five guest to the Catholic mission guest club house for a final send off chat hosted by Father John Georges, the guest list consisted of all the leaders of the different agencies and organizations that had made it at the event. Upon arrival at the missions club house, Pak got a third surprise of the night when he was told that the various leadership would like for him to acquire all the knowledge it would take because they look forward to the day when he would come back and represent them in the Nations Capital as they assure him that in as much as he is going to school on a scholarship acquired by his own effort, they were willing to foot the cost if there was any agreement tying him to the terms and condition of said scholarship. Once again Pak always humble and calm inform the body that he acquired the scholarship strictly through academic excellence and that there was no string attached, he further elaborated to them that his scholarship was a full scholarship which include weekly stipend, he thank them for extending him such cordiality and promised that he will for ever be a part of the region whether or not he had been approached, but he was humble to know that he was regarded in such high esteem by leaders of the region that had only afforded him the ability to serve them, he insinuated that he is more grateful to a region that has allowed him the opportunity and means to be a part of by assisting him in being assimilated in the society.

By the time the night was over Pak had received more offers and invitations then he could ever imagine, one thing is sure he never allowed any of the recognition get to his head, they were all welcomed with praise and said it was the community and it's residents who were the most deserving of all the recognitions that was directed toward him.

Chotas extended his stay in the City of Aberdeen for the purpose of bonding with Pak and for some one on one pep talk on the line of youth leadership before he left for school, as he had promised himself earlier he would not bring up the dirty tricks he was so aware of that was going on with the people around him, because as he put it before, he does not want to spoil this fine young man who has worked so had to achieve all that is be thrown at him on a bunch of back stabbing individuals who won't be able to break his spirit and moral in what ever he decides to undertake.

The days preceding Pak's departure to school turned out to be some of his most memorable days with the people he referred to as family most especially the ones spent with his sweetheart Suzette, to some extent they were almost inseparable, their peer regarded them as a match made in heaven as others saw them as a future political force judging from their deeds even some of the most prominent political leaders saw the two as a force who will be able to do great things, they anticipated that with those two in the mix of the region's leadership there was no doubt what kind of development will blanket the region. On the day of his departure, he and Suzette made a truce.

Pledging one another life long love, he once again reiterated that which he had been telling her, that she will for ever be the love of his life.

Chapter 8

Pak, was once again stunt by the size and population of the environment he had landed in to start his college life, and it took him some time to get adjusted, since for him the largest city he had seen or lived in was the City of Aberdeen, which turned out to be from his judgment at least nineteen times smaller than the City of Boosuk, which turned out to be the size a little smaller than two American Cities combined, Namely; Atlanta in the state of Georgia and Philadelphia in the State of Pennsylvania, because of it's size and many attractions and it's higher institutions of learning together with it's multiple research facilities, Boosuk was a City that was always booming with people from a diverse back ground, as people often said, who every makes it in Boosuk, can make it any where in the World, Now pak could see why, since in fact, the City was comprise of two groups of people rich and poor, there was nothing like a middle class. For a young and up coming serious and focus mind such as Pak it was quite easy to get assimilated into the class of the rich because of his character and his natural human relation skills. It could also turn out to be the kind of city that will lead him in the opposite direction, again; it all depended on how grounded he was in his morals and beliefs.

Pak spent his first week of orientation getting acquainted with his campus environment and signing up for classes related to his studies even though he had not really decided what his major would be, he was quite certain that it would take him a minimum of a semester's academic try out to figure out what exactly he would do, he also was convince that what ever he did was not going to be technology related. He knew his scholarship was for five years and there were no restrictions on what he could or could not do, the level of expectations were his grades for which he was given and depending on his performance, he would be awarded a scholarship to do graduate studies, and knowing him he was pretty sure that what ever it was that he did for under grad he could accomplish in four years if not three.

For this he wasn't the least worried, he just needed to take his time and see what direction he would channel his future which was leaning more in the social science area. And from the days that he wasn't busy with getting situated his mind would constantly wonder in the direction of his sweet heart Suzette, to whom he had written three times in just a week expressing his impatience to be united with her as soon as he gets the first chance, which, was still about six months away to his first vacation, and considering the distance he probably might not want to make the trip, however; when he got to that bridge he would cross it but for now he has to find a way to emerge himself more with the reason for which he had come.

Pak finally had his classes all laid out, and his schedule set fortunately for him, he as a freshman he was suppose to share a room with another student,; an incoming freshman like himself, it turned out the freshman he was paired with did not make it and since it appeared as though he was expected to arrive anytime he was going to be in the room all by himself at least for now, which did not really seem to border him the least, as a matter a fact, it would give him enough time to be alone when the need arises, he considered that more of a blessing than a curse. Another thing that happen quickly for Pak, was his final decision in choosing his major, just when he was nearing completion of wrapping registration, he decided that he was going to be a Mass Communication major with emphasis on Marketing and Publication.

Once he had completed registration, he started to mix and mingle, off course, with a character like his, he could get along with anyone so he made a few acquaintants around campus. It wasn't until his forth week in school that he landed a job in the School's Bookstore as a cashier where he would report to work in between classes and since he had no class on Saturdays, he would work from eight in the morning to twelve midday. Three Saturdays after he started his employment at the Bookstore, he came back from work and there was someone else in his room, since he was not recently informed of his Roommate's late arrival, he was a little shock because he was left out on the specifics of the exact time he would have been in, none the less, he was here and that's the most important thing and now he Pak would have to make some adjustment since he no longer has the room all to himself, he will have to be more accepting and relate to his Roommate as he would want to be related to had he been the one to arrive late for school regardless the circumstances this young man was here to acquire his education just as he had come from nowhere to be a part of this wholesome and life enriching experience and the least he could do was recognize him as a human being and afford him the necessary cordiality humanly possible. The good thing is that even though he had been staying in the room for the past seven weeks all by himself, he had always maintain his allocated section always respecting the space that was for the next person, this made it even more easier for his Roommate to arrange his assigned area in timely manner without having to deal with any unorganized situation that must have been created by Pak as his arrival was being anticipated. When Pak entered the room at first there was no one present, he only got to know because the vacant bed had been spread out neatly and the unoccupied space had been rearranged and stuff put in place as if by some new occupant, he knew right then and there that his Roommate had finally made it on campus, unfortunately he did not know at what time he had arrived nor how far he had wondered away for, but he was certain that they would be exchanging greetings in a few minutes, he must have gone to grab a bite and once he gets back the necessary introductions will be made and they would take it from there. It turned out Pak was wrong for it would be a few more days before he got to see his Roommate, it wasn't until the following Wednesday before he would have the opportunity to lay eyes on the young man who was now his Roommate, a situation that had him thinking all along what was really wrong, and why would he just come and drop off his belongings and then disappear, he was a little scared, but more confused than frighten. There was an air of relief when as he was just about to leave the room he heard the key in the door from the other side, he just sat back on his bed and waited for the door to open and the individual on the other side walked in introducing himself as Debb while inquiring if he was in the presence of Pak.

Pak stood up as he extended his right hand for a shake with his newly met roommate; "you are right on point, my name is Pak and I was wondering if something had gone wrong with you, especially when I walked in the other day an saw you belongings, and didn't see nor hear anything else from you or anyone I was more concerned about what the problem was. I just am grateful that you've finally made it, or are you here to stay this time or do you still have some unfinished business to take care of still?" Before the words could come out of Debb's mouth, he broke into a smile as he responded; "no my friend sorry to disappoint you, whatever unfinished business you had to take care of and you did not do, It's over with your privacy is now compromised because this time I'm here to stay, however you are welcome to sneak while I'm in class or out studying that aside I'm here." He said jokingly to his newly met Roommate and soon to be best Friend, something neither of them knew was about to happen, but judging from the way their conversation was going they both immediately realize that there was some connection going on that they each thought a whole lot was to what was going on between them that is about to give birth to a brand new and rewarding friendship that could imbibe a great deal of knowledge and respect from one for the other. After their brief deliberation, Debb inquired; "what time does the cafeteria closes?" "The cafeteria is open right now, are you trying to grab something to eat? In fact if you ask me I'll tell you that the cafeteria is always open, because I have never seen it closed, even though I'm usually in bed no later than eleven thirty every night since my arrival here, but I'm also up by four thirty every morning and at both times it is always open except maybe it closes at mid night and opens at four in the morning, for me that would be the only logical explanation that I can offer at this time," he further went on to say "hey there's a snack food store at the end of this building which is much closer, and I don't know why they call it a snack food store because it has a lot of full meal in it, in fact the only snack they carry is Tuna and Crackers I guess that's how it got famous before they started doing heavy and full meals."

"Have you tried their meal?" inquired Debb.

"I'm a regular, that's how I got to know, if I'm not mistaking I think by now the folks in there know me now by name, I wouldn't say the same for the food and the people in the cafeteria for the simple fact that I have not been in there since I came on campus." Pak answered.

"What the hell then are we waiting for? I'm famish to the point that I could eat an entire cow, come on let's get moving before I substitute you for the meal." Said Debb joking.

They both walked down the hall on the path leading to the food store, it was at least a seven minutes walk before they reached their destination, just as the were about to enter the eatery, Debb asked Pak a question that he had been anticipating all along.

"If just out of curiosity, and if you don't mind me asking, is there any particular reason why you haven't tried going to the cafeteria since your arrival?"

"Not really, I'm just a little lazy and trying not to venture out of my comfort zone, it's funny that you asked, because the same was just on my mind and worst of all, I have not even made an attempt to go nor has any thing negative come out of there to me, again; I would only attribute it to me being lazy and nothing more." Replied Pak.

"Well maybe we should give it a try one of the days, sooner than later better yet, why don't we do lunch there tomorrow?" Continued Debb.

"That sounds like a plan to me lunch it is, concluded Pak as they walked through the main entrance of the "Snack Kitchen" the rightful name of the establishment they were in. Once inside and judging from the crowd and the movement within, even Debb could admit the atmosphere was friendly relaxed and very conducive, which led to him commenting.

"I love the atmosphere in here, now I understand why you just made one stop and got stuck in as much as I think you should still try another choice since you've got more than one just in case there is a need for change, let alone an emergency." Debb's statement was re echoed, when the menu came and after their various orders arrived, with an additional "Pak you really do have a good taste when it comes to food, by the way, can you cook at all?"

"Thanks a lot for the compliment, I'm not sure if I can or cannot cook simply because I've never allocated time for that, but even if I can the real question is, what would it taste like? Even I don't know until the moment arrives, I don't think that will be any time soon." Pak replied just as they had planned the following afternoon Pak and Debb each found their way to the cafeteria where they had decided to have lunch, and what they found out was even more amazing, because in the cafeteria they expected to be served at a counter stretching from one end of the room to the other, but instead they were faced with various booths of multiple cuisines in them, there were at least seventeen booths in all cuisine from every sector of the Earth could be found therein, all one had to do locate what their crave was and just approach the particular booth carrying that cuisine and it was theirs for the having. Debb was right after all, when he said to Pak it's good to explore in the wake of various choices. The only glitch on this side was the crowd which was on a much faster pace than where Pak had made his usual ritual, unlike the Snack Kitchen things over here were more interesting people more aggressive and far more impatient a behavior widely practiced by the patrons toward the providers and sometimes to other patrons, some thing that most thought had to do with the size of the crowd, even though people did not have to form long lines, and if for any reason there was a long line noticed, additional severs would from a group of standbys be provided for the expedition of service to the comfort and smooth transition of the crowd, one major reason why most people were always in there and kept coming back.

After that first experience the two freshman friends were often at the cafeteria experimenting with different cuisine every time they were in there, and every time coming out with how awesome the food was at every visit, occasionally they still visited the Snack Kitchen, but the cafeteria had taken preference, it also seem they were being noticed more at the cafeteria as well as the Snack Kitchen some attributed that to Pak's constant presence at the Bookstore and it seemed every time he was in the Bookstore his Friend and Roommate would be in there with him, either helping him or them doing school work together, something that even the bookstore manager admired about the two young men who seemed more focused and grounded especially in their freshman year, since the vast majority of freshman came with high determination but once there got lost into pier pressure pose by other in coming students, the party crowd and off course the soon to be dropouts for better opportunity as they will often time put it, as if to validate the reason for dropping out of school with the intentions of making it to the big league without any know how. Due to their collaboration and constant involvement in other campus academic activities, Pak spent less time composing letters to his sweet heart Suzette and more time with the things related to his immediate surroundings, even though he still made it his duty to send her a letter every other week, a far cry for his daily letters which were mailed every three days; at least now he doesn't have to mail them in bulk, now he mails them as soon as they are written.

Pak was still getting all the information and up date that he deserved from his many correspondence with his sweetheart Suzette and Father John Georges, including occasional updates from his friend Chotas from his home town of Sankamaroo, giving him an alibi to inform his friend the kind of human interest projects that he's been involved in, thus sparking his friend's interest in some of the undertakings narrated. Another thing that Pak was making sure of was using his time at work in the Bookstore to make people aware of the different contributions and sacrifices they can make to causes that are so dear to the human race, always careful not to promote just the one that he foster, instead he generalize in his conversation relating to anything that has to do with the development and advancement of morals and dignity in society as it relates to civility. This was also unknown to him making him a little popular among the students; since he was so calm and convincing in his approach, and surprisingly to certain extend, a lot of the students from the upper classes were the ones who would come to him for advice on how they can get involved. He, with the experience and reputation he had already acquired from his completed and ongoing projects put in place before his arrival here, he would always eagerly and willingly offer the best way he knew how. Always cautioning them to do what they are more passionate about and not doing something because everyone else says it is good, rather they should find what they are most comfortable with and go about it cautiously with every energy and fiber their body can provide them with.

Something that was most baffling to a whole lot of people, was he did not have too many freshman showing interest in most of his human interest discussions; a thought he could not get out of his head easily. What then could he do to get most of the younger people to arouse their interest, after all they are the leaders of tomorrow and they need to prepare themselves for what this world has to throw at them, he would think. A thought that he harbored until the day his own friend and roommate Debb confronted him with the question that if an individual who has never had any experience with working with people concern with the various human interest channels necessary to begin the process, or if there were groups out there that one could go to for help in terms of finance and other logistics to facilitate the idea, and if so how can they be reached, and where? This three in one question got Pak thinking how far actually had he gone with his campaign to dissimilate this information, after days of battling with this in his head, he came up with a documented plan in the form of brochures and cassette tape as blue print to be given to every and any youth interested in formulating what is being preached. Having done that less than four weeks, Pak realized an increase in the very group he had hoped to attract rising to an over whelming one hundred and fifty percent, making him very proud of this wonderful and humane undertaking.

Pak and Debb spent the rest of the academic year emerge in their studies and promoting the work related human interest to other students who were ready to be a part of the cause, in the form of periodic seminars, and workshops, and Pak in his capacity as head of the group, was able to solicit aid on behalf of other existing bodies established by him before he came here for School.

At the end of the school year and with a four point zero grade point acquired by both Pak and Debb, and just as Pak had promised his beloved Suzette and Father John Georges, Pak made it back to the City of Aberdeen, where off course he intended to spend his vacation from school and to also assess development with ongoing projects that had been organized by him in the region. He was very pleased with the results he got, and upon arrival, just as he had been given a Hero's sendoff he was also given a legendary welcome when he returned. Above all, he noticed that based on some of the materials that he had put together and sent back from school, played a very important role in bringing a lot of the younger generation to the cause, motivating them to strive harder more than ever before, a gesture which he quietly thanked his Friend and Roommate Debb for since it was his inspiration that led to him preparing the materials. For Pak, vacation did not mean all fun and games rather it was work for there will be plenty of time for fun once you've accomplish your goal. Based on his belief, pak spent the first three weeks of his vacation visiting all the areas he had last visited and inspiring the youth population to see how much progress had been made, and one must say he was the most proud individual on all of planet earth just to see that his words and work ethics had yield fruits more than even he had ever imagine, a feeling that led to him pledging his continuous support to these groups and informing them that as long as they were all still willing to work in the direction ahead, the sky was the limit and positive achievements were just around the corner urging them not to relent, because even though they had come a long way, the longest distance was still ahead, because as he put it if it was hard work that got them to where they were it would take a lot more hard work to keep them in the position they were. Pak was so impressed with the progress he had seen he decided to make a trip to the Township of Sankamaroo to see how they had been doing with their projects, most especially after the move by Chotas to be a part of his sendoff ceremony, and his quest to bond with him for some dos and don'ts regarding the very programs they were undertaking, just to let him know how much he appreciates the idea of desiring the bondage, and this time he was going to make sure he took his sweetheart Suzette along with him; since she had been working and exchanging ideas on whatever the task at hand was since the departure of Pak for school. For Suzette it sounded like a good idea besides she wanted to for the first time take a break to another location for a change even if it was just for a day, but fortunately it was going to be for at least five days and it wasn't going to be all fun because she was also traveling as head of the youth group from the City of Aberdeen, a position she was awarded as a result of Pak's departure for school and because of their involvement in the Nation's youth movement they were regarded as a high power delegation for that reason there were activities and events planned once the word got out that they were making the trip to that location.

Suzette was over joy for the recognition but to her surprise was not expecting the kind of welcome she received. Yes she looked forward to the events that were planned little did she know that there were literally red carpet rolled out at some of the events, not to mention the presence of Town's Executives at every single event they attended.

Because of the warm welcome accorded them, and the work ethics observed, Suzette pledged to constantly revisit and work closely with all involved in the youth activities with or without Pak. After said announcement and in acknowledgement of her kind gesture she was given the key to the Township of Sankamaroo by the Executives and Elders of the town at the same time being conferred Honorary Citizenship to the Township. Due to the hectic schedule and all that was planned during their stay, the minutes and hours seem to go by so fast before they knew it, the time to depart had arrived, and it did not seems like they had done anything tangible, but indeed they had done a whole lot within that brief stay and everyone around them was very pleased with the contribution and sacrifice they had made, just the fact that they had made the journey to the location meant a lot to the residents.

With all the time Pak and Suzette had spent in the Township of Sankamaroo, he saw Chotas on a daily basis but never once laid his eyes on Sojy and every time he asked about him he was told that, Sojy had said that he was in the middle of some venture and would find him before the day is over, an answer which he got for five days in a roll, and at least twice a day it wasn't till the eve of their departure, when Pak's inquiry turned more of a concern about Sojy's health rather than his whereabouts, and when he got the usual answer wanted to know if there was anyway that he could find him where ever he Sojy was camping out at which time there was no acknowledgement of where he really was instead there was a string of speculations, but Chotas and Suzette knew exactly what was going on, because he knew his Father did not really want to face Pak because he was just an evil man at heart and he did not want to face him for as far as he knew, Pak had robbed him of his earthly richest and he will never find it in his heart to forgive Pak. Any thing that had to do with uplifting or promoting Pak he would not have anything to do with it, he would rather support the opposite. Pak on the other hand did not have the slightest idea about what was going on. Chotas had told this to Suzette the last time they were all together in the City of Aberdeen while there attending the sendoff ceremony honoring Pak on his way to start his college carrier.

Pak being the cool calm and collected kind of individual that he is, just thought Sojy was dealing with some personal issue and did not want to be bother with anything external. It wasn't until they got back to the City of Aberdeen that he got a hint of why Sojy did not once make any attempt to even try to see him, considering that he had made such great effort to come find him in the first time. Father John Georges broke the news to him first by first making him to promise that he would not get angry about what it was he had to say about anything regarding Sojy and that he should know before he even heard about his evil intentions, Pak who is also a very jovial person, was smart to read into a statement that carried some heavy weight, so when Father John Georges made him to promise in the tone of voice used, he knew it was serious.

Father Georges first made Pak to understand that Chotas had wanted to let him in on the whole when he made the trip to the City of Aberdeen the last time but because they did not want to dampen his moral made a decision not to say a word before and during the honoring ceremony even when an individual in the seat behind them almost let out the big secret. The priest went on to inform him that it was all because of suzette's Father who did not think anything good of Pak since he was a person from nowhere and he being one of the most powerful person in the City, after finding out that he Pak was from the Township of Sankamaroo wanted to make sure his daughter was not hanging with the wrong person, that's when he started gathering information and really trying to find out who he was and where had he come from? Here Father then started paying for to sponsor the cause to dig into Pak's existence a move which led him into finding Sojy and sponsoring his trip to the City of Aberdeen to verify his story, and what was in it for Sojy? There was for Pak an inheritance from both his Mother and Ninuh that could sustain him for his lifetime and since he Pak was still a minor and Sojy was still Ninuh's husband he had to be the one responsible for him until he was old enough to manage his own affairs. So it was no coincident that Sojy had made it to the City of Aberdeen, he did it because he wanted to prove that he had not done anything to Pak and to also let the people know that Pak was doing well and it was all because he was being given the best of care due to his (Sojy) involvement in Pak's life. He further explained to him that the trip made by Chotas should have been made by Sojy, but when he was approached he flatly refused and Chotas was so mad and upset about his Father's attitude that even when the trip was paid for he wanted to sabotage it by pairing with Chotas on a budget for one to make it work for two a move which to this day he Father Georges learned that the two men are not even on speaking terms, since Chotas ran away from his Father just so he would not make the trip for Sojy's low down and dirty tricks he made Pak to understand that Chotas felt short of revealing this to him because he could not easily workup the nerves to tell him. But Suzette knew about it from the onset due to loyalty to her father she too could not bring herself to tell Pak about it either, above all she did not want to loose his trust and confidence hence she decided to let a sleeping dog lie. Father John Georges, after revealing this to Pak took a keen look at him for the first time and sensed that he had touched a nerve in the young man sitting across from him whom he thought he knew so well but then realize that he did not know what to think, he had never seen Pak like this before ever and in as much as he wanted to continue with some of the most intricate part of the story which had not been revealed he thought to stop and continue at a later time, after Pak had digested the first segment, at this juncture the Man of God made him to understand that he can only imagine how hard it would be on Pak but that should not break his moral, considering that he had already survived some of the worst ordeals in his life and that this is just another chapter of life that he would have to accept and move on. Pak only requested that he continued with the details.

Chapter 9

Pak never really recuperated from the fact that he was kept in the darkness by the woman he thought he loved so much whereas he had confided in her about his entire life, he felt betrayed a feeling which ended up putting a strain on their relationship making them to spend far fewer time together than he had expected. To crown it all off, Chotas was back visiting the City of Aberdeen to touch base one more time with Pak before he left again for school, but this time there was no holding back on the story the way he wanted to tell it the first time and it was easier for him to do now, and he did not hold anything back, as hard as it was for Pak to endure he sat through it all because he told Chotas not to hold anything back including the involvement of Suzette and her family to use him as an apparatus for their experiment.

Two weeks after Chotas left Father John Georges got word for a transfer to Booscum, where he was going to be managing the region including that of the City of Aberdeen, his transfer was to take effect immediately and in three days he had left the City of Aberdeen for his new assignment Pak who still had three and the half weeks to his departure date for school, and with the state of affairs that he was experiencing with the new revelation involving Suzette, and in lieu of an excuse, he just decided to make the trip with the Priest, being he had already spent a year in Booscum for school he could help his mentor the Priest get settled in, and to put a little distance between him and Suzette together with her family in the main time, as he absorb the entire story . They arrived in Booscum safe and Father Georges loved it given that he had been here before on a visit that lasted not more than five days at a time, he thought it was a good idea that he had been afforded this transfer together with the title of regional priest, but just as he was getting ready to settle in his new position, not even one week in Booscum, he was asked to leave the Country and take up a different assignment at the Vatican in Rome a much greater position, causing him to spend less than two weeks at his assignment in Booscum, once again leaving Pak by himself, and like always Pak thought to himself he has survived worst and this is just another segment of life's many tests that he had come to endure, he was very sure that he would again strive and conquer, a thought he would later realize that even he had under estimated, since this time he had more on his mind than even he could harbor, after all the mind is strong but it is also a part of the human mechanism, therefore it has it's breaking point, and one never knows when they'll get there and what will actually happen once that time comes.

Father Georges departure did not help Pak's plight, because his friend and roommate Debb was still on vacation and it will be another week or two again before Debb arrived on campus, and unlike the first time when Pak newly came to Booscum, when he could think about nothing but the daily communications and comforting letters to and from his sweetheart Suzette, this time all that ever came to his mind was the way he felt he had been sold out by her and the betrayal he felt he had endured at the hands of Suzette and her family, even though he knew that her father in the beginning of their relationship didn't seem so pleased about it, her father had once physically confronted Pak and told him to get the hell away from his daughter Suzette or he might regret his involvement with her when he wakes up one of these days in a world he has never seen before.

Even as the thought linger in his head, he thought to himself, that they had all made amends and decided to let by- gone be by gone, but learning the full detail and the negative vibe that was planted for the satisfaction of some evil individual just to boost his ego it was a disheartening thing to note.

With all this on his mind, and the persistence of depression for the first time in his life, Pak's emotions got the best of him and led him on a path that others thought he would have taken much earlier in his life when influential individual in his life and was there to make a difference started dying as if from some plague unleashed by nature to target those closest to the young Pak.

He decided to try some stimulant to get some sleep, and even though he had never done anything of such before, he jumped in full force; experimenting with alcohol, marijuana and a little bit of PCP (angel dust).

From the first time he decided to travel on the path of destruction, and as strange and awkward as it may all appear to be, he still kept up his good grades, only now he was no longer an "A" and "A+" student, instead he had drop down to a "B+" and an "A" student.

Pak was so good and charismatic he was able to convince his friend and roommate Debb to start using, and frequenting the places that Pak went to reload on his supplies.

Once Pak got started on the path of destruction, not even the mind moving and comforting letters from his mentor Father Georges who had started to noticed some changes in Pak once the story of betrayal was narrated to him, but there was far little he could do since he had been reassigned, and to add insult to injury, Pak was on a full scholarship with room and board being a part not forgetting to mention books, he did not have to pay a penny out of pocket for anything regarding his college education, all he had to do was show up and make the a minimum of a "B" average. For this reason, Father John Georges thought, there was a lot at stake for Pak, or else he would have made a way for Pak to have traveled along with him and continue his education in Rome, it was all a pointless idea, besides he was enrolled in one of the world's most reputable institution. Above all, he had in the past seen Pak survive situations that were by far worse than what he was going through, and he was certain that Pak would once again overcome.

It took him three semesters for Pak to finally recollect his right bearings and exit the path of destruction. During the days he was on that dangerous path he also became a big womanizer, his love life duration were on a weekly basis, some way somehow, he could not stand being with one girl more than eight days, some of his relationships lasted only for the weekend come Monday morning he would be seen with another woman, and to add on to that, Pak had also become a part of the party group dragging his buddy Debb along the path of destruction with him. Debb who himself was doing well in his studies, was also not exhibiting his full potential just like his best Friend and roommate, he too like Pak had also become a womanizer, even though he was not as rampant and profuse.

It wasn't until when Pak had paid a visit to his mentor and friend, at the request and sponsorship of Father John Georges in Rome during one of his midterm break, that the priest noticed a great change in Pak, a change he did not suspect because it was not reflected in his letters through their weekly communication, it was in that instant that he lamented to Pak that, in as much as it is good to confide in people it is not good to allow people to shape your destiny and he thought no one else knew that better than Pak who had experienced so much in his young life that made him stronger than most adults he had encounter, he further made Pak to understand that even he had been amazed during their first encounter, and that he had also learn a lot since the first day their path crossed, and he has never stopped learning and exploring greater and better grounds, he said to Pak; As you already know Pak, you have a lot of people that are looking up to you from the organizations formed by you and remember the speeches that you were asked to deliver? " Before Pak could answer, the priest butted in.

"There is a lot of people young and old who wake up every day, and feel blessed because they were a part of the group that you spoke to and above all knowing that you turned out to be the good from the ashes of ruins brings peace to the minds of all those that were under your voice including me, you might not believe this but it's the truth and I did not think that what happen back in the City of Aberdeen would have had such an impact on you, had I know I would not have told you, I guess I should admit that I'm guilty too. Both you and I know that we can not undo what has already been done, we can only correct the mistake and build on the good, remember you said that in one of your speeches? You might want to retrospect some of your own speeches when you're sometimes feeling down and low." It turned out Father John Georges really knew Pak, because that pep talk was an awakening call for him and his life after that took a turn for the better, it brought back the Pak that every one once knew after three semesters of absence.

When Pak finally came back from vacationing in the great City of Rome with his Friend and Mentor, Father John Georges, every one who for the last three semesters had been thinking that he was a soul that had been lost due to the epidemic of university misfits, had to think twice, because just as he had turned from being a perfect child to a junky, he was back in his shell and doing exactly what most of the people who knew him the year before he started misbehaving, he was now back to himself as he was once known to be, his first order of business when he got back a week before the start of classes, was, to meet with the very group that he was always hanging out with doing the things that he had no business doing in the first place. This time instead of getting drunk and high on controlled substances, he was on a mission to talk them into reversing the habit and do the opposite, stay on the path of sobriety, and just as he had persuaded his roommate and best friend

Debb to join him in living free of drugs and alcohol, even though it took him longer than he had anticipated, but he got the job done.

The actual achievement of his mission of getting his peers to do the right thing, was, at least seventy percent of the party crowd turned away from the path that would have led them on the broad boulevard of destruction, and cause them to flush their bright future down the drain. Pak however did have a regret that he did the best he could to put in the right column of life, and it turned out to be a female friend that he had been fooling around with when he was in the life of drug and alcohol abuse, not only did he notice her beauty, she was equally talented, very smart and a well calculated individual. Now that he's back to himself, and has exited the life of drug and alcohol abuse, he wishes he hadn't been the one to lead her down the path of destruction, for she is now dead as a result of a drug over dose, but all that is now behind him and Lord knows he will forever carry the life of that individual on his shoulders.

As a result of the transformation, and the manner in which things were going, most of his peers anticipated that Pak would have been the one to be the student leader during his senior year, instead he made it quite clear that he would be a strong support of the student government in every way possible, but he had no intentions of being the head, a wish that was also taken and well respected.

Just as he had promised, when the Student Government was formed, Pak really was a strong supporter to the extend where he was even named advisor to the Student Council President a role that he executed very well, while conducting his usual role as a youth advocate conducting and establishing more youth programs, thereby creating more opportunities for the active and passive members, of all that was going on, people could really see Pak for the kind of leader that he was. In his efforts to make things right for the mistake he had made, he vowed to himself that never again will he try to hold any thing against anyone, no matter how offensive it may be because life is to short to dwell on one tiny mishap in one's life when there are many days in life that one needs to rejoice for as oppose to staying mad for a very short life that we have here on earth, he, in that decision made up his mind to make amends with his one time love and best friend Suzette, even though he was no longer interested in a romantic relationship between them, he did not want to go through life being enemy with her either, after all they were once best of friends, and could still hold on the good of those memories shared by them.

Not only was Pak a strong student advocate during his graduating year, he was also highly respected by the administration and faculty of the university, for he was one person who was seen by both groups to mediate on the part of either party, considering his status as a student that was such an honor for any individual no matter which side one was, knowing Pak, this was not only an honor but also a responsibility which required a maximum effort of sacrifice dedication and the ability to make critical and life changing decisions which he did not take for granted. He also used the position to spear head his crusade for the abstinence of drug and alcohol abuse by the youth of the day because as he usually puts it, a lot of our brilliant colleagues could get misdirected into areas that would not be beneficial to our world, since every breathe is responsible to make a difference in an environment that we inhabit. From our ancestors, and are expected to deliver it to those who are to inhabit it after us, not only in the perfect condition that we received it in, but if we can, make sure it is delivered in a more refined and developed stage.

Pak functions in these various roles still did not deter him from being the valedictorian, graduating at the top of his Class, but long before graduation, and before Pak thought about doing taking on the responsibility of being an intern, quite a few leading journalistic and media firms were doing the best they could to secure his employment with them, although he was very excited about the idea of a job security upon graduation, he also thought that with enough experience on the job and a little capital he could be able to do exactly what most of the giant advertising firms did, and it would be such a great idea if he had some cash to start off and then he could just sgo from there.

Pak was able to finally decide on an offer by a global media firm after reviewing the many options he had received base on the recommendation, advice and consent of his mentor Father John Georges, who had made it his business to personally go to a branch of the "Media and Graphix World Wide", an International Public Relations Firm which had it's head quarters in Zurich Switzerland, in quest of an internship position for Pak while he was still in school, even though he Pak had no idea that the priest was behind the scene making sure he got as much practice as he could to prepare him for the job market upon graduation, which was achieved as the Priest had imagined, but something that he did not really foresee was that Pak would like to be the navigator of his own future, and he would welcome any path that could possibly stir him in that direction with no harm or any form of danger to his person or anyone connected or not connected to him.

Pak was again well loved and respected by his bosses and co-workers because of his dedication and commitment to duties that were assigned to him during his internship, an attitude which even as an intern helped secured a permanent position for him if he decided this was what he wanted. When he was made aware of this development, Pak made it his duty to work even harder to the extend where the branch manager asked that he served as administrative assistant to him a position which could afford him a good grip on the day to day affairs of the establishment, because according to him he had seen in the young man a high exhibit of leadership ability and if he really wanted to, he could become a regional manager or overall president for the company with offices in Zurich. He executed his duties so well at the point where the manager would constantly seek his opinion when there was an important decision to be made, not surprisingly during the third month of his internship, he was introduced to the President on his first and only visit ever made by any high ranking official of the company from Switzerland, aside from being introduced Pak once again made an impression on the visiting executive, who due to Pak's performance regarded the Branch one of the most productive and well organized he had visited in the last three years he had served as the overall President for the Company. Before his departure and after learning that Pak was only an intern who still had two more semesters in school, and there after will be going for an other eighteen months for graduate studies, he personally conveyed to Pak that should he ever find himself in Europe and decide that he still like to work in the media world he should be sure to look him up, and in conclusion he told him he had a very bright future in this line of work and it would be more beneficial to him to continue and keep up the good work he had so rightly exemplified.

After being given such high marks by the Company's President on account of the performance of Pak, even his Boss at this juncture had an added value to the dignity and respect he already had for the young man so poised and well grounded, as a result he was named the first and only intern in the Company's history ever to be given the employee of the year title, a nomination which came with an economic size car and three months of reserved parking. It was later learned that the recommendation to name Pak employee of the year, came from the visiting President during a one on one section with the General Manager who actually happened at the time to be the Regional Manager overseeing every establishments of the Company in the Middle East and West Africa.

{ Chapter 10 }

While Pak was on the roll with his duties and maintaining a hectic schedule he and his best friend and roommate Debb were still chatting on a daily basis on the events that had unfolded during their work day. Debb had also secured an internship with another media firm, and was also being taunted by his employers for a full time position though not as big and established as the one where Pak was, but it was the most established local media firm without any fancy foreign connections not to mention leadership, his Firm was all home grown, and he too just like Pak was doing a very great job, and was being commended by his bosses just as well.

The two young men grew into adulthood since being freshman and working passionately on each other's projects when the need arises neglecting whatever rivalry that should have existed between them considering they would have been soliciting the same clients, one thing they always maintain was the loyalty to the secret of their respective establishment, that aside they were constantly in competition for the same client, whenever that occurred, Pak would be the victorious one for clients who were more flashy and real flamboyant, Debb on the other hand came out victorious for most of the up and coming and stream lined budget conscious establishments, so they both in their own right had their following and they were also loyal to the people they served, and they were still in school even though it was just a matter of months to graduation for them both.

Graduation for the duo was eminent, as a result they were both preparing for grad school, Debb, for his part had already accepted a position with his Company while continuing his graduate studies. Pak told his Boss that he was not yet ready to go full time with the company, he rather asked to stay on as a part time employee since according to him he had a full plate dealing with his many youth groups and various projects with regards to intensive advance studies, and that he should be allowed eighteen months, at which time he would definitely be ready to settle in a contracted position for a duration of a minimum of three years not to exceed five years on the first agreement, it might be longer the second time around but for now it will climax at five should they agree on the same terms, a suggestion well taken by his Boss with the belief that he Pak's future employment with the company was eminent, for that reason he decided to give him as much time as he needed to make up his mind. Pak on his part really was still undecided, nonetheless, he would wait and see what happens after grad school, since in fact his Boss had granted his wish.

Debb and Pak were thinking about a joint graduation party on the Saturday after their graduation, since the main day of their graduation was on a Sunday, when Debb cross path for the first time with the infamous Suzette who was somehow responsible for Park's derailment from the positive track of life when he made that detour in the direction of the much talk about alcohol and drug life taking a lot of his friends and peers with him, even he Debb was shock when this beautiful lady walked straight up to him and called him by his name, because he had never seen her before, he knew that for sure, for a beauty like hers, can never be missed, in the event where it is missed, it will never be forgotten and that was all the reason why he was so positive that he had never laid eyes on her, so when she walked up to him and said.

"Hi Debb, you must be a little tired from working all those long hours and still have to put up with School work?"

He turned in the other direction to make sure that she was really talking to him, and when he turned back to face her with a surprise and puzzle look on his face, she did not give him time to answer, instead she continued.

"I suspected that would be your reaction, anyway we have not formally met, my name is Suzette, and I want you to know that all that you must have heard of me, could have been wrong or a little exaggerated, I advice that you give me a little chance to get to know me, and you will have a whole new opinion about me when Debb finally got the chance to address her, the words that came out of his mouth surprised even he.

"I'm very pleased to make your acquaintance, I must also inform you that your beauty is breath taking and further elaborate to the elevation of any negative conceptions I must have had about you, there's none, even though you broke my friend's heart he really had nothing evil to say about you, he only felt betrayed by love, and that he says does not warrant bitterness toward any particular individual, instead he said his heart was too little and he allowed it to wonder in the world all by itself."

Suzette upon hearing those words felt so relief and a need of obligation to see if she could once more fit into Pak's world as she did before. With that thought in mind, she decided to let Debb know her full intentions for showing up after all this time.

"I guess you might also be wondering why I'm here?" before Debb could answer, she further went on to say, I'm here to show my support and to let Pak know that he will always be the man that I respect whether he decides to have a relationship with me or not, after all we were best of friends before we were lovers and I still hold those precious memories dear to my heart, and to that what I've decided to do is to host and sponsor a graduation party in his honor, and I just pray that he'll accept." Debb was not too sure what Pak would have thought of the idea, and for that he did not want to be too inviting nor did he want to discourage the idea, all he said was, that it sounded like a great idea, but only Pak would be the best position to validate that, which she understood herself, with great hope and optimism.

Finally when word of Suzette's intentions got to Pak, he could not help but think how fantastic the idea was and coming from Suzette it meant a lot to him, considering he did not give her chance to really put things in prospective, instead he just took off and left simply because he thought he was betrayed. Pak and Suzette finally got the chance to meet before his graduation, and that was when she revealed the last leg of her surprise for him.

Just as he had thought earlier that he was a new person, fate also had it's intention for him, once he met with Suzette and they both exchange apologies for what had transpired, Suzette told him.

"Please don't get mad about this, but Chotas has been trying to reach you for the longest through me and he said he wanted to meet you one on one to convey his regrets and frustrations to you regarding the situation, even if you did not want to see him anymore, all he asked, is one last chance."

"I would love to meet with him just as we have, as you rightly know, due to my own selfishness and stupidity, I did not really give you guys the chance to explain yourselves which over time I've seriously regretted, but all that is in the past and I'm ready to make amends." Pak said, to Suzette's surprise, and this time when she spoke, she felt she was communicating with the Pak that she knew in the City of Aberdeen.

"Now that you've said it, I want you to know that Chotas is also here, and he said even though you decided not to stay in touch he made it his business to be at your big day and just say congratulations to you, and also thank you for making him a better person than when he was growing up."

Pak at this time was even more impressed with what he was hearing because it was also his intention to reach out to everyone including Sojy who had been considered the worst person in this entire scenario, not just for them to be present at his graduation but to ease himself of any grudge that he harbored for any form of evil against him. So when he heard from Suzette that Chotas was present he felt real good and wanted to see him right away.

"Where is Chotas right now?" He asked "I'm not sure if you'll be able to see him any earlier than five hours from now, because less than forty five minutes ago, he told me how tired he was and had to go get some rest and that he'll make every effort to see you first thing tomorrow morning, at which time he would be well rested and can sit and talk for the longest."

"Well I think you're right, if the man needs his rest let him have it, after all the body can only take so much and no more and when a man says he's tired, he has to take heed and listen to himself and his body, because if he doesn't the body might end up shutting down on him and no one wants that, I guess I'll see and talk to him tomorrow than." He said reluctantly.

"But how have you been? How are your Parents, and how are things in the Great City of Aberdeen?"

Everybody's fine they all send their love and congratulatory treat and say after all said and done they still see you as a Citizen and Resident of the Great City. Of Aberdeen, there are plans underway to erect a symbol in your honor and to allocate a parcel of Land to be fashioned at your discretion, you will be properly informed when the time comes as a matter of fact, the Mayor of the Great City of Aberdeen is expected to be here during the commencement ceremony, I think he wanted to be the one to inform you of that grand decision, no one else knows about it except my Dad and he let it slip out when he and I were talking this morning, so remember you did not hear it from me."

"I won't say anything, to your Dad or anyone else on purpose, but do not blame me if it slips out just like it did to you from your Dad." Pak responded jokingly to her cautious statement they both just laughed over it truly speaking, I don't think I deserve such an honor, because of the little things that I've done, as far as I'm concerned there are people who are more deserving and have done far more greater things to make a difference in the lives of a cross section of the residents and the Community of Aberdeen that made it the great City it is known to be today and these are the people who deserve the recognition or should I say a front row seat I can't imagine, how me of all those prominent individuals got so lucky to be counted among the chosen few and should that ever happen I will always remember to say I'm a product of those great shoulders that I have yet to measure up to, for it is those shoulders that are my foundation "just like you Pak, you are always a very grateful and modest person, you may not realize it but you made a difference in a lot of lives and that alone is recipe for a commendation." Suzette told him they sat and conversed for a little while longer talking about everything including what they had both been up to in their personal lives, it felt so good to them both they decided to have dinner together just to celebrate their reunion and the appreciation that comes with good understanding, even though they were no longer romantically involved, but just as they concluded the appreciation of a good friendship should never be tarnished or impacted with the emotions of a romantic desire. Suzette at the end of their soiree, decided to invite Pak, over for more discussions, an invitation which he respectfully declined.

After escorting her about ten feet out side of where Suzette was staying, Pak came in just to find his buddy Debb waiting for him with the another good news, this time it was from someone that he did not even know, but because of a life that he had touched there was a fantastic present waiting for him whenever he wanted to pick it up. "I have been looking everywhere for you," Debb was saying to Pak as he approached, there is a group of people waiting for you in the theatre's lobby and they have been for at least two and half hours, something about your influence on the life of a son of theirs which lead to an entire community benefiting from the good lessons learned, that which came about because of you, and that there is something that they would like to do, to forever keep you in the memory of their community, but they need you permission to perform what needs to be done.

"Do you have any idea where these people came from by any means?"

"They did say, but honestly I don't remember." Replied Debb.

"Thanks for the message anyway I must find them now or else I might not be able to see who they are anytime soon, by the way would you like to take the walk down there with me?"

"Unfortunately, I'm having a meeting with the freshman media class in three minutes, I would love to but this takes front stage for now, besides they might want to have you all to themselves, in the main time good luck." Debb added "One more thing I think you already know what's in store for us from the camp of Suzette, since you did talk to her before she got to me, I think they're planning to make it real big for our graduation." Pak was saying as he walked away from Debb, in the direction leading to the theatre where his guest had been patiently waiting for him to join them.

Pak met the waiting entourage in the Lobby as he had been told by Debb, it turned out it was the very last group he had addressed before his freshman year in college, and since he did not remember the exact phrase or phrases that led to this group coming to see him on this day, he felt honored and grateful for the lives that he had touch during his deliberations with these various groups, and every time that he was approached by any of these group, brought relief and honor not just to him but every positive individual that helped shape his journey in life, for without their support encouragement and love he would not have been able to be the person he had turned out to be.

It's such an honor to have you folks here to celebrate this glorious and noble milestone, I cannot begin to find the words to express my pleasure for a sacrifice of this nature on your part, I can only express my gratitude by informing you that whatever it is that I've achieved on this day is due to the encouragement and support I have enjoyed from you humble people who when all odds in life had given me the red flag, you still believed in me and allowed me a space in your hearts which led to all this all important triumph."

"Pak, truth be told you are the person who have made all the necessary sacrifices, especially when most of your peers were thinking only about themselves, you were designing strategies and blue prints for others to have what some only dream off, and as we can all see, your accomplishment today, is not just for you but for every path that was laid by you for the development of our people." Came the phrase from a very slender and beautiful face in the crowd who at first he did not recognize, but as she spoke the words, he realize that this is the young lady that was at the head of the group who had shyly greeted and introduced him to the audience when he went to address them, she had grown to be a bright and outspoken individual he thought. He also remembered that this young lady, was very athletic in three sporting categories at an early age, a combination which set the stage for a greater and brighter future for this young and talented individual. As the thought crossed his mind her name was immediately triggered from the bank of his brain, and when he finally spoke it was the first word out of his mouth.

"Vero" he said to her surprise, "I did not recognize you at first, he continued, you have grown to be such a beautiful and outspoken individual if you don't mind the compliment, I'm highly impressed by your evolvement, are you still as athletic as you were back when I first met you?" He inquired making the discussion more personal while acknowledging her "I'm surprised you even remembered my name since there were so many people around you, you've really made me to feel special and have a whole new different regard for you as a person this lets me know that you weren't addressing your audience as an orator, rather you did see the looks on people faces and the scenario you demonstrated came from your heart and they were all real as we related to them at the time you delivered them, you will forever remain my idol." She concluded.

"Thank you, Pak replied, but again as I said before hand, it is and has always been people like you who kept me going and once more, by your showing up here today another form of inspiration even if I had no vigor to want the positive attributes in life I would be so energize to the surprise of the word energy itself. The honor is and will always be mine to be a part of whatever projects and developments initiated by you, especially when it comes to human resource advancement, and development."

Pak who thought he had not done the group of nine enough justice at this juncture, put on his thinking cap and said.

"In appreciation of my gratitude for this noble move on your part, I would like to express my heartfelt thanks and say a big welcome to all of you for taking time out of you busy schedule to be a part of this mile stone."

He spent approximately forty five minutes to an hour with the group getting acquainted with some of it's new members and discussing matters of relevance relating to some of their achievements since his last encounter with them, and when it was time for him to leave he left once more with a renewed sense, that life should never be taken for granted, because every individual has an impact on every individual, so it's always a good thing to consider others when you make your decisions in life for you never know who you will impact. As he turned away and bid the group a farewell, even some of them felt more impressed and relieved that they had had an opportunity to be a part of this noble task, and being in his presence was an experience worth their while, as he was not only a man who knew the down side of life, but had been a full participant of some of it's tragic attributes, and for him to come out on the positive side speaks huge volume.

It was Sunday, the day of graduation for Pak and his classmates, before eight o' clock there was an exodus of people from different walks of life and a huge fanfare on the campus of the University. Along the route leading to the main building where the commencement was to be held, human traffic was moving steadily, and judging the crowd everyone seemed to be happy to be a part of one of the Country's largest Universities not forgetting to mention one of the World's most renowned Universities, highly recognized for it's production of renowned doctors lawyers statesman and most especially for diplomats, for it is often said that if not all, most leaders of global organizations, such the United Nations, League of Nations Organization of African Unity, Asian United for Progress just to name a few, do spend at least one semester there before acquiring full diplomatic status on the global front.

It turned out just as the crowd descended for this great mile stone Suzette was not the only one planning a surprise for her former lover and best friend Pak, and when she found out that there were other groups planning the same event she made it her business to have them all merge and organize an extravaganza, little did they know that what they were in for, was a huge undertaking and that it would last far longer then they anticipated, whether they were up for the challenge remains to be seen.

Chapter 11

There were lots of acknowledgements by the various speakers on the podium during the graduation ceremony as usual; the entire program lasted three hours for some it was eternity but for the graduates, it was an experience of a life time after all their struggle and hard work leading to this great milestone.

Pak who happened to have been the Valedictorian for his class gave an articulate and powerful mind moving fifteen minutes speech surrounding the struggles and successes he had encountered along his path in life leading to this fruitful and rewarding venture and when he was done with his speech, as he retired from the podium, there was a huge applaud follow by a standing ovation that even he did not anticipate, leading to some emotional tears streaming down his cheeks, whether in memory of the faithful departed in his life or just the ups and downs we will never know. But one thing for sure he's not the individual who will come to tears easily so for some who really knew him could not help but exhibit a little teary eye most especially the female counterpart present. He was again greeted with another round of applaud and standing ovation when he was call up to receive his diploma.

When it was all over with at the end of the ceremony people were everywhere, even though the program lasted three hours it took another hour and the half to finally rid the location of the crowd that was present, navigating a lot of the people to other parties that had been planned to climax the activities of the day, some graduates asked that their party be deferred to a later date but for others it was now or never and among those now or never parties was Pak who really had little or no input other than to accept the generosity of these individuals who had held him in such high esteem beyond his own imagination, because knowing him and his level of modesty he would have requested a tiny celebration with a hand full of close friends and those he considered as family; such as Father Johns who had played a major role in his elevation to this great and gracious achievement who had also vowed to any and every one he had come in contact with that he would not miss Pak's graduation for anything in this World he'd even joked at one point in time that if it was to fall on the day that he was to be called from labor to rest, he would ask the angel of death to give him a few hours extension just for him to see Pak receive his diploma for the bachelor degree in whatever area of studies he had decided.

After the grand events of the day leading to all the hype of an alcohol tobacco and drug fill evening, people everywhere were ready to start the following chapter specifically the businesses that were considered to be the direct recipient of the apparent financial success of the weekend which leads to at least a twenty five percent boost to the local economy. Graduation here every year is a big deal and every civil and public servant residing in this City of distinguished education (Student Center) knew just what it meant to the Central Government and the residents of This Great Town.

For those who knew it so well, prepared for this week end as if they were preparing for the Christmas Season as this was also the weekend the eyes of the World will have a microscopic view on this tiny Global Educational District of excellence and perfection which also gives local leaders a chance to brag of their stringent and impeccable academic contribution to the World as a whole There was also the sound of loud music on every street corner one turned, and there were people everywhere as if the graduation ceremony had left the campus of the University and transfer to the Streets of the City but this time without the podium and the ceremonial lines of the various platform guest addressing the crowd in an orderly manner which had now been replaced with interrupted conversation, dancing and everyone else trying to talk above the crowd and music that would keep them from being heard creating more noise and confusion then any one in their sound mind body and soul, as it always turns out be people would also decide to speak in unisome and it was definitely at one of these many parties that Pak and his group of a planned surprise graduation party were going to be and most of the people who had once met Pak that were also present at this location of the World currently would find it very pleasing to identify with the young man at this point and time in life.

Everything turned out to be such a blast during and after the hours of the graduation and the Monday following the weekend of the graduation the City's only international airport and the various transportation hubs were busy with individuals from every aspect of life trying to find their way back to the area they called home, giving this great academic City a final taste of their economic growth contribution for the end of this year's financial dispensation. It was at one of these transportation hubs that Pak once again found himself alone with his Friend and former Lover Suzette along with others expressing his gratitude for the huge surprise she had carried out for him he just could not believe that this was really happening after all he had gone through in his early stage of life, a realization that made him think of his Mother and all the wonderful people in his early childhood who were not here this day to share this all important moment with him as he thought somewhere beyond the grave there must be a group of individuals giving him thumbs up for a job well done and now more than ever before he was ready to make the best of life and take advantage of every moral advantage presented to him in life; not that he didn't before, or with less appreciation, rather this time it will be with a lot more value and appreciation.

It turned out she didn't have to leave until two hours later and they had both sat for about thirty seconds without a word when finally she suggested "you know I really don't have to leave today and I could be of some help to you as you put your things in order and prepare for whatever the next chapter you wish to undertake if you don't mind because I know fully well that you could use the help, and please don't think that I'm doing this to get back together but I know how hectic it is and you could use all the help you can get, and for old time sake I'm offering you my help with no strings attached." her voice seemed to have been coming from a far distance and as though in a trance was back to reality out of his world of dream and illusion to give a spur of the moment answer to a sporadic statement. Surprisingly, he found himself giving an affirmative answer, an answer not even he could believe "I could use the help. But when are you expected to leave?" He heard himself saying as if it was a question coming from someone else. "If you don't mind your presence would mean a lot to me right about now I earnestly don't mean to ask that much of you considering; none the less I think right now and here I would not want to be with no other than you." A statement that baffled her with a ton of disbelief, at least not from him more so that a few months ago he didn't even want to have anything to do with her and everything to do with everyone else. What if she hadn't try every effort she had to get in touch with him would this moment ever had arrived? She thought to herself, this time it was her time to come out of her trance when she heard him say " If we must do this we need to start now because I know there's a lot to put in place and you might want to leave at some point in time I guess we better get started before you change your mind and I'll be right back at square one."

The two left the terminal and before they could make to their destination they stopped along the way to grab a bite; because of the load of work they anticipated that was waiting for them they both decided on a meal to go. They were barely at Pak's Apartment when he finally said to her. "I really must apologize to you for my behavior after all you were only trying to protect me and I didn't realize that at the time I was more concern with my own selfish thoughts and the only reason I never reconcile our differences earlier on, is ego and today I owe you more than an apology. Not only didn't you relent but you showed up from nowhere with so much vigor and vitality to organize such an extravaganza for someone who had given you nothing but grief and heartache that you did not deserve in no way shape or form hence forth I promise that I will never again betray your trust and confidence for as long as we both shall live and this Suz is my sincere and earnest pledge to you I will do everything I can to make it up to you I only hope and pray that you give me a second chance and if for any reason you decide not to I will not blame you because I understand that I put you through a lot and your satisfaction and concerns must be taken into consideration, I only pray that you give me a positive answer."

When Suzette finally spoke her voice cracked and with tears rolling down both of her cheeks she said; "Pak I will always love you no matter what and there is not an ounce of malice or hate in my mind for you, just hope that we did not through the trying times that we both went through, because it almost cost you everything I'm so happy that you were able to bounce back from the ordeal and still turn things around. Let me tell you if you haven't noticed, you have been and will always be my hero what I've learned from you as a person and a leader is priceless and I could not have acquired from my Dad even though he's rich and influential you on the other hand may think you are not rich but what you have is better than any riches and except you decide that you don't want to be but you my sweetheart are destine for greatness. You may not know it now but mark my words one of these days when we are both up in age you'll say to me remember what you once told me, it has come to pass." At that instant they were at Pak's Apartment and he was turning the key in the front door, once inside they lock into each other's embrace hugging with tears still streaming down her cheeks when suddenly they were engulfed into the best kiss they ever had the entire time they were lovers neither could describe the feeling nor tell anyone the duration but one thing was sure they would both admit that it lasted for ever and they wish it never ended but that kiss also led to the most passionate sex they in their entire time on earth had ever had sending them into a rest that lasted for at least three hours they woke up almost the same time and started from where they left off and when it was all done, it Suzette who spoke first.

"I realize today that you called me Suz and it sounded so good it made me blush inside I almost jumped at the sound of it. Could you tell me when exactly you came up with that beautiful short for my name? Cause as you know I've never heard it from you before."

"I'd always long to say it to your face and see how it will make you feel and since we are just turning a new page, I think we just need to start everything at fresh on a new note if it is alright with you" Pak replied.

"Pak in as much as I like the idea of the new name I want you to know that the Pak that I knew then was my Idol and he remains to be the same person, he may have graduated from college yesterday, but he is still that caring and dedicated young boy I first met in the Great Township of Aberdeen always focused, forward pressing and never scared to explore because it was your quest of exploration that led you to Aberdeen in the first place at that and not knowing anybody or where your next meal will be coming from yet you were not perturb by the unknown and you made it your business to arrive any way and once there you made your presence felt how many of us at that age can say something of the sort. Fast forward look where it has led you today; do you see what a role model you are ? Some individuals where only here to celebrate your accomplishment and mind you, they had never met you but based on what was said about you from others and your courage and strength in life about the dedication you exhibit when you envisage a cause or project. Let me tell you my friend if you haven't noticed. You are not only a hero to me but to countless others who have seen, followed or heard about the progress you've made thus far. Your journey My Love has been a remarkable one above all it has been a blueprint to countless others as we speak this moment, there are a lot of people out there trying to do everything like you did." Suzette stated and took a brief paused, and when she resumed with a teary pair of eyes Pak handed her some tissue from the box of tissue that was on the head of his bed "Pak!" she continued. "Even if you never again in life made love to me ever I'm pleased with these last few hours I'm spending with you because you My Love are a living Legend and how often do people come in contact with Legends especially coming from the Geographic Location of the City of Aberdeen, look at you the eyes of the entire World were on you as you addressed them from one of Global Academic Cradle during your graduation ceremony. Tell me, if that is not legendary then; what is?"

In search of words from what he had just heard from her, now was his time to be baffled by her with your emotional moral and physical support and it would not have been accomplished without your involvement so I want you to always cont yourself as a part of whatever it was that you just said because individuals like you create legends who produce good results and because of you the

Universe will always be a better place for us all to share. And just to let you know the short for your name just came out, I guess I'm more matured and ready to be more romantic with the one individual that I've and will always keep a special place for in my heart and if you don't mind I'll like to pattern the short and make it my exclusive if that's alright with you."

After that brief conversation between the two, neither could believe what had come over the other after a nasty split which first left them bitter then forgiving and now back to being the other's confident, best friend or better yet lover. But whatever it was they both realize that they had both landed on new grounds and this time it was meant to last considering the fiasco that had just transpired over the past few months.

When he spoke again, it was in relation to his current state of affairs.

"I'm famished; I could eat a cow aren't you?"

"When we walked in we were busy exploring one another's body and forget we brought something to eat, I think we can eat now after a rigorous session of love making and rest. Your Royal Highness, if you don't mind let me do you the pleasure by getting you fed would you like us to eat together or do you want to eat separately? We could eat out of the same container so we don't have to make a whole lot of mess on top of what we already have to clean up." Suzette asked while walking toward the area where they had placed the food they had bought on their way in.

"I really don't mind, as a matter of fact it makes a I love having to eat out of the same tray with you." Pak replied Suzette came back with the tray carrying what they had bought earlier and they both eat in silence and after they had finish eating, she dumped the remaining food and disposal tray in the garbage.

Suzette and Pak at that instant decided to spend some time together after a passionate and emotional afternoon. After all it was the usual three months holiday for all schools in the country and it wouldn't do any harm to extend the breakup and makeup moment after such a romantic session.

At first, Suzette had decided she would only spend two days with Pak but in her message to her Parents, she did not specify any time all she said was that she would be a little longer than what she had anticipated, she actually ended up spending one and the half weeks with Pak. During which they were inseparable and it ended up being the best time they had eve r spent together as a couple ever. Three days to her departure, she received the biggest surprise from her Sweetheart while at a local diner.

She had excuse herself to go to the bathroom and when she got back her sand wish had a gold color napkin saying read me and when she sat in her seat and picked up the object he immediately went down on his knees saying.

"Suzette, Will you marry me?" as the contents of the napkin were revealed to her.

With no hesitation she replied

"Yes! Yes! I will, I will anytime!"

Tears streaming down her cheeks "Now I'm really glad I stayed, what more can a girl ask for? Not in a million years would I have imagined this, and if this is what you get for attending a former lover's graduation, then I want you to keep graduating." She said in a very low tone where only he could understand as her voice cracked while the observers clapped in commemoration of what they had just witnessed.

When he finally spoke, she thought she could sense tears in his voice even though they were not visible, she could tell that he was also shedding some tears on the inside.

"This is just a token of my appreciation and my pledge to protect you for as long as we both shall live. But above all for putting you through unnecessary pain and suffering and I want you to continue being the best friend to me that you were when we were much younger and I will forever remain indebted to you because you are the confident that anybody would ever wish for, don't you ever allow anything less."

As he was concluding his statement she broke into a smile with her eyes focusing over his shoulders, and he realize that he was looking past him at something behind him when suddenly he heard the voice.

"There you are, haven't seen much of you both almost forever when was it? Let me see it was at the party just before I left town for my two Weeks vacation when you both disappeared and had everyone asking me about you or is it just three days ago when I got back and being constantly informed about areas that you have been spotted by everybody but me?" He continued jokingly.

"Debb!, Welcome back My Friend and Brother how have you been and how was your vacation? Aren't you kind of early? I wasn't expecting you until next Week and as you can see since graduation and while you were away, I've been very busy with two fruitful and rewarding ventures straightening up my new apartment and of course as you can see, playing host to my newly engaged fiancée Suzette I proposed and she accepted; meaning I'm off the shelf and she has been spoken for by me and please make sure to echo that to everyone including you " He concluded joking.

"That is very beautiful Pak, look how far that thing glows. By the way I'm glad you did because if you hadn't I probably would have done it for you by her permission. I am so happy for you two I don't really know how to express it in spoken words. I wish you God's entire blessing and pray that he keeps you both together even during eternity."

"Thank you good Friend I'm happy that you are happy because you need to start preparing your tuxedo as we might be coming up with a date in the next forty eight hours since you will be my Best Man I'm also looking to ask Father Johns to officiate as I suspect Suzette will approve since he has been an intricate part of both of our lives."

"Father Johns will love to be a part of this, as you already know if it left to he alone we would have been married by now and I personally wouldn't think of any other but him, I'm sorry we did not make the decision while he was here for the graduation." Suzette butted in.

Debb join the duo and they sat and chatted for some time discussing everything from their various backgrounds and the different path they had each travel in life laughing and giggling over some of the silly things and seriousness on some of the really bad events, off course of the three Pak had some of the most gruesome as it relates to tragedy and misfortunes. But he was also quick to acknowledge that with the mishaps came some good things in as much as he as an individual with the help of others and the two that were there present. As a matter of fact he always considered himself very blessed because for all he knows the early childhood was dealt a very nasty blow and by the grace of the Almighty he was able and led to make some adult decisions even when he didn't know what the outcome would have been yet he pressed on and was able to be in their mist. What else could he has done differently?

And as sad as it may sound, "Besides having grown up without any biological parent I wouldn't change anything because if I did then we will not be sitting here today I probably would have been a spoiled brat and waiting for them to baby sit me always. Not that I would not have resisted, but both of you know how imposing parent can be sometimes even though they think they are doing it in the interest of the child at times it becomes very boring to the recipient. I guess for parent it makes a whole lot of sense since they are suppose to look out for the well being of their offspring."

Debb on the other hand was saying. "As for me I see it a different way Pak as we already know there is a whole lot of peer pressure growing up and I think parents do a good job trying to keep their children in check, cause if not a whole lot of children will go astray, one of the very few who in the absence will make such sound and rewarding decision in the on their own as a child, you are just a very special person and your kind are hard to come around. And even if one did survive opportunity are often hard to surface for people who find themselves in your shoes that my friend is one of the reason why so many people have such high regards for you because you are not only special you are THE CHOSSEN ONE my dear Friend and Brother, everybody loves you for no reason just the mention of your name brings joy to a whole lot the sound of your voice attracts a mountain of attention. How many people among us or who graduated with us can say the same? Above all Pak as good as everything may sound on your end, you keep excelling because in your pursuit you tend to be very much humble, some other individual may allow that to go to their head but not you and that's the reason why I highly believe that God is the one guiding you along the way."

"Come to think of, I never really thought of it that way Debb, but you are so right and you sum it up so well no one could have done any better, and let me say this I'm so glad that I'm a part of this all important conversation and better yet I'm so happy that I have been added to this package that has been divinely designed for you by the Almighty God." Suzette implied with a little humor.

They sat and chatted for another then left the diner headed for Pak's new apartment where they stayed until ten pm that night discussing the wedding between Pak and Suzette not really reaching the conclusion on any particular date, for Pak had earlier said that it was going to be left to him to come up with the date later and then have a pep talk with Suzette for her approval.

The following day they had decided to again hang out together since Suzette had only one more day to be with them and they were going to make the best of this togetherness. It was during this time that Debb for the first time met a beautiful young lady name Marie Nukes who was very much delighted to spend the afternoon with them not so surprising Debb ended up falling in love with the young lady the minute she sat to converse with them and made sure that she was going to be his girl friend before Suzette left something that he made clear to both Pak and his new fiancée Suzette, a statement that was never doubted or looked at as a bluff by Pak because he knew the capability of his friend and once he made up his mind to get something done he will definitely go after it no matter what where, who when or how once it has been accomplished before he will make every effort to do what has once been done. So when it came time to escort Suzette to the train station where she was expected to leave for the great City of Aberdeen, Marie was there to see her leave it turned out the two girls had a lot in common and the both came from a very strong moral back ground with Fathers of high influence in the community in which they reside and a size of wealth that could last at least four generations after them with a lone daughter to inherit whatever they've accomplished while on earth. Once the two started talking and realize they were so alike it seemed like they had known each other for a life time.

When Suzette left, it seemed as though she took a part of Pak with her, he had never missed anybody so much in his entire life, but the good thing about the entire scenario, they had agreed that she would be gone for just a week and she would be back to spend the rest of the vacation with Pak as they put finishing touches on the final plan for the date of their wedding and then they will both leave to meet with her Parents and let them know what they had in mind for the preparation of the big day. This off course was Suzette's idea not that she didn't think her Parents would approve, she just wanted to have a heart to heart with them and acquire some girly advice from her mother and they can both together sell the father on the idea not that it would be difficult because he would support her in anything she decides to even if he does not think it's good, he would only make sure he air his caution and tell her what he thinks is right and let her make the decision as he would always conclude no matter what I say to you, you'll always do what you decide on what you want and so far you have not disappointed me in your decisions making but as a parent I will always have my reservation about things you decide to do even if they are good; she also knew that beside what happened before concerning the Pak incident with her father would never again be repeated because he had apologize to her several times regretting that he was the cause of them breaking up and had once wish he could personally get them back together but ego had prevented him from approaching Pak on the matter. But one thing is clear he had also once declared Pak as one of the finest young men on the face of this earth, and that any woman who he ends up with him in life will be a lucky lady. A declaration he has made both publicly and privately so coming to the realization that his only Daughter will be that lucky lady would definitely bring peace to his heart more so that he has watch him excel and conquer life's ups and downs. What people don't know he was the instrument behind the organizing of the graduation batch spending time and money behind the scene making sure that all is well and perfect because it is a gesture well deserved for such a fine Individual.

For the week that Suzette had gone Pak spent every single day thinking about her while he was preparing for her return at the same token arrangement to make it more female friendly good thing he had decided on a two bedroom two and a half bath not even knowing that he would be sharing it with his special someone but that is so like Pak always thinking ahead of things even if he doesn't know what will happen he always makes room for the unexpected for as he usually puts it. "If one can afford, it's better to have it and don't need it than to need it and don't have it since everything in life is borrowed and the only thing that one exits this life with is what one puts in the brain in the form of knowledge acquired and the food that one puts in the stomach to sustain the body strength and muscles while we breathe this breath."

Pak with the help of Debb and Marie had done a great job in putting the apartment together the only part of the apartment that was not fully ready was the extra room which he and Suzette had considered guest room, he had put a queen size bed along with a dresser mirror in it since he was not expecting any guest anytime soon maybe he wanted Suzette to be the one to fix it up since she is the female and would be the one most concern with who's staying in it.

It was a great surprise when Suzette and her Mother showed up unannounced at the apartment a day before she was expected; it also turned out to be a delight for Pak who had missed her so much beyond expression. The Mother and Daughter team arrived just before eight o clock pm that evening with the Daughter insisting on going to find a hotel room a decision that was frown upon by her Mother implying that she was her Child and where ever the child spends the night, should be the same area where the mother spends the night, even if it cost the mother to sleep in the living room on a couch she should, so there should be no worry about the parent because that parent can take care of themselves, as long as the Child is happy that parent should also be happy for the fact that the parent is there because of that particular Child, and it was a good thing that there was an extra room with a bed all that was left to be done was put some sheet on the bed and a set of pillow and all will be alright after the lodging situation had been settled, it was Suzette's Mother who spoke.

"My husband Pak , is very delighted to learn that you have chosen our Daughter Suzette to be your live time partner, and even though he is not here right this moment I must assure you that I speak for the both of us and that's the only reason why he allowed me to come and see what necessary preparation you young people are making and how soon without taking over from you because it is your day and your decision and in the end you will only have you both to relate to for all the support in the world, all we are trying to do is provide you with a road map which you might not even need because you've both been very responsible in your dealings, and as a result of parental concern we just want to assure you that we will always be there all you need to do is call, and we will come running."

Suzette was also for the first time hearing of her Father's approval because when she told them about the engagement he did not say whether or not he was for or against it he only offer his congratulations with no anger or excitement it was as if he was not ready for her to get into something of that nature, she finally on her own concluded that maybe her Mother must have played the convincing role until she heard it was his idea that she makes the trip back with her and make sure to inform Pak that they could not have wished for a better Individual of his status and integrity, and after the information delivered that evening they all went out including Debb and Marie for dinner. The following morning Pak his Fiancée his future Mother in law all three went to get furniture for the guest room at the request of the Mother in law and at her expense, she told Pak to consider it a graduation present, little did he know that was just the beginning of a string of surprises to come as a result of his marriage proposal.

Her request was granted and the guest room was designed and set up to her liking, it was on third day after they had decorated the room to her liking they came to the apartment from having dinner that night at the diner where Pak had proposed to Suzette when there he was standing at the gate of the apartment complex patiently waiting for them Suzette's Mother Liz, said; "I see you made it I was hoping that you would arrive earlier tomorrow, I'm glad that you made it, none the less I've been having a blast with these two love birds and you're about to find out for yourself at first hand."

After she laid eyes on her father she was positive that he had really approved of her be the future wife of a young man that he had had so much doubt about at one point in time, but she was also happy that he had change his mind and is willing to accept him as a future Son-In-Law. While on the outside her father did not say much other than I'm glad I made it I can't believe I've made two trips here in less than a month just to make sure my Little Girl is alright and having the time of her life. That was when Pak greeted him and said.

"I didn't know you were here quite recently." He kept his response for the right time.

They had all gone into the apartment and made themselves comfortable when suddenly there was an alarm at the door when Suzette's Father said.

"That must be my luggage."

"I didn't know you had your luggage outside" Pak said.

"I didn't" the older gentleman replied.

"He had them delivered." Suzette's Mother said.

"Now that you are both here we really need to get a hotel." Suzette said.

"I don't see why family should visit family and not want to share the same roof besides this gives me an opportunity to get better acquainted with my future Son-In-Law, I know this may come as a shock to you Pak thinking I did not approve of your relationship with my Daughter. The fact of the matter is I've always respected you as a young man growing up but when I found out that no one really had any concrete facts about where you came from I was a little nervous something I do not expect you to understand today but one of these days when you have a Daughter of your own you will understand what I mean. That my young man is behind me now and I just want to ask that you forgive me for that and let's start a new chapter, that also was the major reason why I attended your graduation uninvited and unannounced I really didn't want to spoil my Daughter's joy, by the way I also want to commend you for a great speech, you my friend are destine for greatness and I will die happy knowing that you are the one that takes my Daughter from under my roof. You also have my full blessing even though you have not said anything to us officially yet but from the ring and what she told us I'm happy to know that you feel that way about my Daughter that's the reason why I stopped everything I had planned to make this trip and made sure her Mother accompanied her here , cause when I heard that you were planning to make the trip, I told myself one way I could start making up for my probe on your life was to first save you the trip and let you know how much I accepted your gesture toward my Little Girl and suggest to you that since you are going to be here, have her transfer her credits and acquire her degree from the same University as you that is if you or she won't mind I just think that would be great." By the time he ended his statement it his Daughter who was most surprise of all; because she did not know that her Father had so much respect for her in that regard as he never had such discussions with her, he would rather have them about her and with her Mother rather than to have her directly involved even though it is her life. Based on what she had just witnessed she developed a whole new respect for her Father, one that she will forever cherish, from that point on everything about discussion for that evening was in the form of thought until it was time for her to go to bed.

Suzette's Dad had never been a man of many words so he really was making history with his audience here present, and when he finally completed by directly addressing Pak, it made the entire session more authentic and viable.

"I'm in a state of shock, I had no idea you thought this highly of me, and this day before God and man I promise that I will be the best husband to your little Girl any woman in the world could ever wish for I will never disappoint you for the confidence reposed in me.

Right at that instant, Pak's future Father-In-Law rose from his seat walked up to Pak and gave him a very firm handshake as he said.

"Son I've known for quite a while now that I can always count on you to the extend where I can even trust you with my life, and that's the reason why you have me in your home and sharing the fruit of your labor with the two most important women in my life , not even they have gotten this much confidence from me with all the family time holidays and celebrations but seeing the kind of individual that you are, and should anything happen to me I would want no other than you to take over my family."

Suzette and her mother were so over whelmed words were inadequate to express their emotions instead the two Ladies just sat and allowed the tears to stream down their cheeks in expressing the joy that gratified their hearts from a speech of the most influential male in both of their lives.

When the two gentlemen parted hand shake, it was Pak's time to respond.

'Sir I'm at your command, who am I? to question such generosity." Not another word out of Pak when he made that statement as if to say a word to the wise is quite sufficient. The two ladies couldn't be happier for the choice of their new male figure as appointed by the current one.

After that huge session they all spent about five days together leaving the entire routine to Pak for his direction including things that were to be taken care of by Suzette's Father as if it was a dress rehearsal.

They stayed with Pak the entire time until it came time to leave when Pak was informed that Suzette was going to the City of Aberdeen to straighten up some family paperwork and that she should be back in less than two weeks again with her mother.

They all decided to leave when it was to go, Pak who was told to stay at home and do what he had to do did not take them to the station where they were suppose to depart from instead he just

Kept Himself very busy, while awaiting word from their departure.

It wasn't because he did not receive ay message that had him more worried, it was his instinct that had him the most on edge, he had had this feeling before and it is never good when he starts to feel that way; cause in his young life it had occurred twice and every time he was faced with adevastating and sad news. At that very moment there was a knock on his door, and when he opened up the door there was a police officer and a strange lady he had never seen before.

"Sir, there was a serious car crash and we have three victims in the hospital on critical list, we have been informed that they came from this address…."

Pak did not hear another word after the word address when he butted in saying

"Is anyone dead will they be alright what hospital are they right now?" Asking all three questions almost immediately. When the female that was tagging along the officer replied "They are at the University Hospital Sir, and we can definitely take you there if you so desire."

Pak was at the Hospital's intensive care unit waiting room for at least two hours before he saw Debb and Marie walk in; it would take another seven hours of resuscitation while Pak and his friends were locked in a session of hope and prayers before a female doctor emerged, expressing her sorrow for the young lady involved who had died on impact and saying that it was too early to say whether the elderly female and male were going to make it she explained that they were in a pretty bad shape and had been put on life support until their condition were stabilize before they could start any serious treatment.

Suzette's Father was the first one to gain consciousness after eleven days in a coma, although weak and frail he recognized Pak almost immediately who had been at the hospital Everyday since he got the news of the accident occasionally going home for a change of clothes and to grab a bite, he also had the support of his friend Debb who made it his business to spend a vast majority of the day with him while his girlfriend Marie took care of things they trusted her with.

Pak who had been previously advised not to say anything to anyone of the victims in case they came out of the coma was not sure what to say when confronted with his Father-In-Law to be coming through from a period of coma which seemed like eternity, but with some stroke of luck there was nurse instantly as if she had been summoned in the room to take care of the situation explaining to the elderly gentleman that he was in the hospital and that he had been in a nasty car crash which had put both he and the elder lady in a coma, and before she could utter another word, he slipped back into the coma, that will last another seven days in the main time about thirty Minutes after he had slipped back into the coma Suzette's mother had come out of the coma and was wide wake fortunately for her the Doctor was making her rounds when she came through and since she was in a much better shape, she was given the full detail of all that had happened including Suzette's passing due to the accident.

Suzette's Mother "Olivia" on her hospital bed was force to make some critical decisions, including the one to hold off the burial of her Daughter until she was strong enough even though she had fully recovered and in a perfect shape body mind and soul to put things in prospective with the hope and aspiration that the Father will come through and be well awake to be a part of the process, a wish that came to pass.

Archie; Suzette's Father who had finally come through really did not gain full recovery since the accident left him paralyzed from the waist down, but his mind was as sharp as ever before only relying on a wheel chair to move him around that which he used to go to his Daughter's funeral and because of the nature of the accident and the individuals involved, there was not even enough room to stand not to mention that there was not a single dry eye in the entire place, and when Father Johns who should have officiated the wedding between Suzette and Pak took the pulpit to preach

Suzette's funeral it made the pain and cries even louder than anyone could imagine a moment which lead to a teary and emotional moment for the clergy man who had never in his entire time in the priesthood been seen like that before, ever! being a mortal being we all have feelings and some of the things that impact us the most in our individual lives, and this was Father John's moment that even he could not conceal no matter how hard he had tried and it was at that instant that the audience started to notice the choking of words due to what he felt and by the time he descended the pulpit the loud outburst of cries could be heard from every angle of the occupied edifice.

Pak, Archie and Olivia despite Suzette's death stayed in constant contact maintaining the relationship that Suzette anticipated had she lived for them to be married, and it all came about as her Father decided he knew that what his Daughter would have wanted. A gesture that was highly welcomed by the Mother but who after two years of the accident started to decline in her health including contracting the Alzheimer disease causing her to occasionally forget who Pak or Suzette's Father was, Archie on the other hand and apart from the wheel chair was alert more than ever before.

As for Pak he could not come to grips with the many time disaster had struck on his end especially when there was a major change at the end of the tunnel in his mind. As an adult one would think that he would have gotten accustomed to the many losses he had endure earlier on in life, but the hurt this time was more than when he was much younger simply because now these were people that had formed a part of him for quite some time unlike when he was a child and too young to process some of the things that happened back then.

For a good while Pak decided that he would not get too close to anyone else, for fear of sudden death and to make sure he did not greave for the lost of another that all relationships would be strictly business, just to later on realize that no matter how cruel life can be, it needs death to complete the circle of a the human existence leading him to the conclusion that where live exists death is definitely at the end of that tunnel waiting to make it's presence felt.

Chapter 12

Pak used grad school to stay below the radar and mourn the lost of his beloved Suzette, because of that he was rarely seen and not too much of him was heard instead he put all his energy into developing his mind for the challenge that was ahead of him, and when he finally emerged it was as though he had never left in the first place. But this time he was more mature and ready to face not only the uncertainties of the world that life has to offer rather to accept that at the end of life there is an individual or something called death and that every man woman boy or girl born on earth by a woman will someday have to come face to face with it at the appointed time, for this reason it is very important to make the best of life cause one it is gone it is gone. Even with that thought at the back of his mind he still did not think he was ready to have a real serious relationship meanly because of the lost that the living feels for the dead.

His professional life that he had spent in undergraduate school carrying two majors, Business Administration and Journalism, on the other hand was without blemish and he was enjoying every bit of it with his best friend and Debb partnering with him on a pat time basis. His romantic life took a hit in a direction that was not actually to the liking of lot of female especially the ones who ended up sharing his bed with him nothing lasted longer than a month and no one had any actual strong hold on him for he often said "What is not permanent let it circulate" and as far as he was concerned he was not permanent, when it came to romance so he was in complete circulation but not the kind of recklessness one that he once practice back then when he was pursuing his first two degrees. So when he decided to go solo and do his own thing Debb tagged along and was ready to everything it took for he knew that whatever his buddy Pak touched professionally turned to gold and he didn't want to be left behind for they had been friends far too long to work along and erect an empire out of the aches of nothing, as Debb often referred to Pak as "The Constructor" and that was when they both decided to have their own P.R. Firm to compete with the already many established ones where they rose to the very top of the list with the strategies designed by Pak. His initial strategy was first and foremost, to offer a real steep discount as compare to others and acquire all necessary information about the particular client's interest in respect to whatever.

They have to offer the public be it product or service, then use a street team that he had organized to launch a massive survey whilst at the same time connecting with other firms to find out rates and other competing devices used in their line of business, thereafter he would then make maximum use of the electronics and print media this attitude and relentless effort of his paid off making them the most sought after ad agency in almost half of the English speaking World, and by the time a lot of their competitors could realize what was going on he had climb so high to the top they could not help but follow his lead.

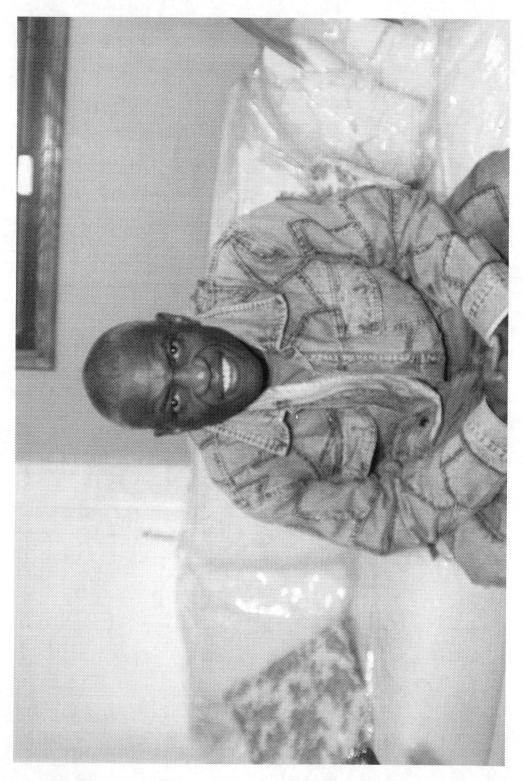

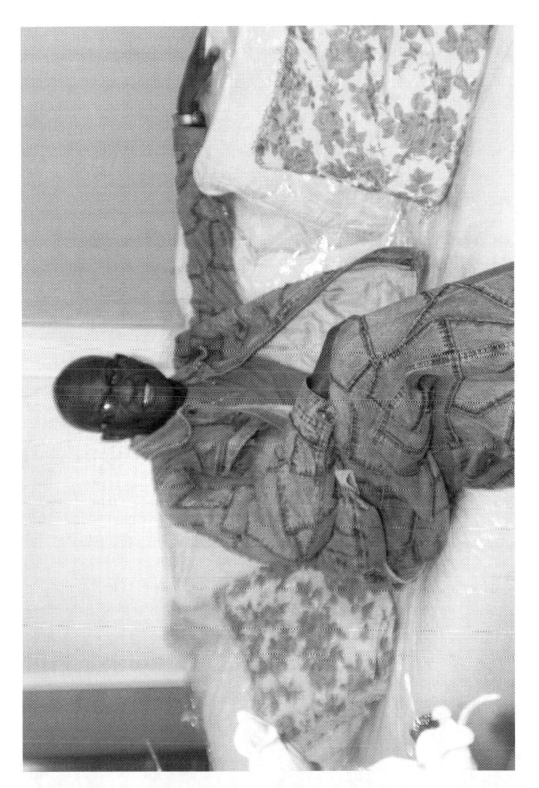